Spirit Sight
Short Stories

by Jennifer Carole Lewis

Spirit Sight
Short Stories

by Jennifer Carole Lewis

Whispers in the Dark

Rose on the Grave

Third Eye Open

The Spirit of the Holidays

Text copyright: Jennifer Carole Lewis Whispers in the Dark 2015 Rose on the Grave 2017 Third Eye Open 2019 The Spirit of the Holidays 2017 Cover copyright © Samianne Art and Jennifer Carole Lewis

Edited by Cait Gordon of Dynamic Canvas
All rights reserved
Printed in the United States of America

Published by Past the Mirror Publishing.
ISBN: 978-0-9940121-6-6

Also by Jennifer Carole Lewis:

Books of the Lalassu
Revelations
Metamorphosis
Inquisition
Judgment
Division

Special Investigations
Deadly Potential

To everyone who has ever heard a knock in the night, a mysterious footstep or an unexplained voice.
I do believe in ghosts.

TABLE OF CONTENTS

WHISPERS IN THE DARK
PAGE 11

ROSE ON THE GRAVE
PAGE 79

THIRD EYE OPEN
PAGE 185

THE SPIRIT OF THE HOLIDAYS
PAGE 265

WHISPERS IN THE DARK

#1 Spirit Sight

Light and music poured out of the open door of Big Ray's. Being the only source of nightlife and alcohol for fifty miles, this rural bar offered exactly what Greg Cooke needed: a chance to blow off a little steam after staying under his parents' roof for the last week. He might love his mother and father, but he hadn't lived with them since he was seventeen. And now he remembered why.

It had initially sounded like a good idea, especially after he'd let Janet keep the apartment when their two-year relationship fizzled out in a toxic mixture of incompatible schedules and polite conversations. Their building was right next to the hospital, and he didn't want her having to drive anywhere after a double shift. His home-contracting business took him all over the city and surrounding townships, so it didn't really matter where he hung his hat.

Then his mother called, complaining about knocking pipes and flickering lights in their fifty-year-old home. He promised to take a look, and she offered to give him a rent-free place to crash while he sorted things out. *Save money, help out the folks. It should have been a win-win.*

13

Except he hadn't slept well once in the week he'd been there. The pipes didn't just knock, they could have been part of the STOMP tour. And they did it at all hours of the bloody night despite his efforts to muffle them. He'd replaced more light bulbs, fuses, and wiring than he cared to think about, and there was still only a fifty-fifty chance of any given light staying on or off in accordance with the switches. The frustration frayed his temper. Greg found himself snapping at his father for tapping and scratching while restoring furniture, or ready to bury his head in a pillow to drown out the smell of his mother's stress-baking. Other people loved the scent of fresh bread and cake, but to him, they were linked with some of the worst moments in his life.

Shoving it all into the back of his mind, he walked into the bar, determined to have a good time. It was full of truckers, bikers, and pretty waitresses in tight clothes. *Good enough.*

He ordered a beer and got himself a decent seat, one with only a few strips of duct tape masking cracks in the vinyl covering. A few of the bikers looked like they might be eager-drunk enough to welcome a fight, but after they got a good look at Greg, they backed down. At over six and a half feet, a lifetime of hauling construction materials and tools gave him a physique that discouraged even the most bloodthirsty MMA-wannabes. Add in the shaved head, and he had a virtual "Not A Good Idea" tattooed across his forehead.

Two more beers followed the first, but none of them were helping. He was debating whether or not to head home when someone stepped through the door.

She was gorgeous despite the dusty clothes with long light-brown hair pulled back in a ponytail under a baseball cap. Her pretty heart-shaped face featured bright wide brown eyes, and her lithe figure promised softness in all the right places.

She went straight to the bar and ordered. One of the truckers started to head over, but Greg glared at him until he thought better of the idea. Ditching his half-empty bottle, he sauntered casually toward her to order a refill. The woman sat there, smiling to herself and tapping her fingers against the bar.

Damn. She had dimples. Now he really was hooked.

"You look like you're celebrating," Greg remarked.

"I had a really great day at work tonight." She gave him another flash of those adorable dimples. "I got a full corporeal manifestation on my infrared. Not the clearest representation, but I'm sure I can clean it up with the digital editor."

He listened to her rattle on, arms waving in gestural description for whatever she was talking about. He couldn't make heads or tails of it, but her excitement was contagious.

"After I packed everything away, I was too jazzed to go to sleep. So, I thought I'd come here and blow off a little steam." She smiled again. "Enough about me. What brings you here?"

"More or less the same. Though it sounds like your day was better than mine, at least until tonight." He leaned forward.

"What happened tonight?" she asked. He studied her for a moment. She seemed genuinely curious. Could she really be oblivious to how attractive she was? Either way, he didn't intend to waste the opening she'd given him.

"I met a gorgeous woman who lights up the room with her smile."

The smile in question could have powered the city for weeks, so he kept going. "It turns out she's smart and interesting, too. Now I'm starting to think this is a pretty good day, despite the crappy start."

"It's not how you start. It's how you finish." She lifted her beer for a toast.

"Agreed." They clinked bottles. "Only one thing could make it more perfect."

"What's that?"

"I'd like to know your name," he teased.

"Jessica Miles."

"Greg Cooke."

Jessica drained her beer and looked at him, tilting her head to one side. She leaned in close, running her hand along his chest. His body leapt to instant attention, swelling behind his jeans. He'd never reacted so strongly to a simple touch, not since he'd been a teenager. When she licked her lips and tilted her head up, he knew he was a goner.

She kissed him, her lips sweet and light against his. He wanted to push her up against the bar and grind his hips against hers while he plundered her mouth and explored her body, but he kept himself in check. This was exploration, not an explicit invitation.

He wasn't made of stone, though. He pulled her in tight and let his fingers trace the contours of her firm ass through her jeans. He teased her mouth with his tongue, and when she opened her lips under his, he plunged into her. He felt her shudder and clench with pleasure under his touch before she drew back.

"I've never done this before but, would you like to come home with me?" Her voice was low and husky with passion.

"Damn straight." She didn't need to ask him twice. Home turned out to be a tiny little apartment. Colorful scarves and strange abstract pictures covered the otherwise bare walls. Stacks of books were piled neatly on the shelf below her computer. The only part he really cared about was the bed, which he was pleased to see was large and soft enough for what he had in mind.

First things first, the baseball cap had to go. Her soft honey-brown hair fell around her face and across her shoulders in a silky tumble. She flashed her dimples at him, and he did what he'd been dying to do since he first saw them. He kissed the first, right beside the corner of her mouth, and lightly ran his tongue over it. Then he began to nibble his way back along her jaw.

She tilted her head to the side, granting access to the precious nook between her neck and her curtain of hair—the secret cave, which held the perfect first-stop sweet spot, the sensitive join of neck and head, just below the ear. The moment he brushed it with his lips, she shivered and pressed closer, hands clinging to his shoulders.

He teased the little spot, working it with hungry kisses and light nibbling. Guided by the soft hitch in her breathing, he knew he'd found the right combination. His cock throbbed with each taste, ready and eager for a turn.

She wasn't shy about exploring him in turn. Her hands slipped up underneath his shirt, tracing and shaping the contours of his broad chest and shoulders. His rucked-up t-shirt impeded her and was starting to restrict his movements. Reluctantly breaking away, he hauled it up over his head and tossed it in a corner.

To his surprise, she turned the tables on him rather than encouraging him to go back to what he was doing before. She moved in close and began to press lingering kisses along his bare chest. He let his head fall back and buried his hands in her hair, enjoying the quick darts of her tongue licking and kissing her way across his skin. She drove him wild as she let herself sink lower and lower, tasting his abs.

He stopped her when she reached for the button on his jeans. The touch of her fingers brought an eager surge to his hardened flesh, and he didn't want to risk a premature ending to the evening. Instead he wrapped his fingers in the hem of her shirt and gave a light tug, checking with her before moving forward.

Nodding approval, she looked like a wanton sex goddess with hair tousled, lips swollen, and eyes half-lidded and dark. He took a smug moment to enjoy the fact that he was the one who brought this out of her. He carefully stripped her out of her shirt, leaving her in a clinging bright-purple bra.

Bending her back on the bed, he kissed the tender skin along her stomach, letting himself inch upwards toward the hidden breasts beckoning them. Her hands urged him up while soft moans escaped her lips. She was close. He imagined how wet and hungry her sheath would be for him. He could feel the rhythmic clench of her muscles under his fingers.

He peeled back the bra, revealing a beautiful pair of breasts. Her nipples were tight and flushed with a rosy glow, begging to be tasted. He bent over and took one in his mouth, sucking hard and deep. The sudden switch from gentle to demanding wrought a sharp cry and an arched back. Her hand clamped onto his head, pinning him in place. He pulled deep, rolling the beaded nipple with his tongue.

"Oh God, yes"—she panted—"More." He couldn't resist any longer. He slid his fingers beneath her jeans and panties. She was still arching against him, unaware until he slipped one finger between her nether lips. Dripping with passion and heat, she cried out when his finger brushed past her swollen clit. Her whole body began to shake and buck against his, shouting out her orgasm.

He tweaked the sensitive nub, prolonging the explosion of pleasure. She shook and shuddered, riding his hand to satiation. Releasing her breast, he pulled back to allow her a few moments to recover. She lay sprawled half-naked on her bed with his finger still caressing her inside her jeans, breasts heaving with each shuddering breath. He could still feel eager aftershocks trembling through her.

"Wow," she whispered when she finally met his gaze again.

"We're only getting started," he grinned, retrieving his hand to undo his jeans.

Her eager smile only encouraged him. He pulled her up off the bed, letting her straddle his bare lap. His rough calluses caught on her silky skin and hair as he shaped her body with his hands. She ran her fingers over his smooth skull. Their mouths tangled together, trading hot and hungry kisses. He fumbled for a condom with numb and clumsy fingers, all of the blood having relocated to other body parts.

Slowly he let himself slip into her warm and welcoming depths. He couldn't suppress a grunt of satisfaction. She echoed with a soft hum of encouragement, rising up and down against his thighs to pull him deeper and deeper.

Although he loved watching her ride him, he wasn't about to let her set the pace. He lifted her easily, keeping himself buried inside as he lowered her onto the bed. She clung tightly to him, her nails digging deeply into his shoulders.

Leverage back on his side, he began to pound into her. She lifted her hips to meet him thrust for thrust. When she arched back and screamed in ecstasy, he joined her, bellowing his release.

The two of them collapsed together into a sated tangle of limbs and bedclothes.

Jessica woke up alone, blinking sleepily at the afternoon sunlight slanting through the window. She vaguely recalled Greg explaining he had a job to do this morning. It might have been a textbook line, but she believed him. Her instincts rarely steered her wrong when it came to people. They'd certainly been on target for last night.

A grin stretched her face even as a lovely echo of orgasm rippled through her core. Whatever the man did, he knew his way around a woman's body. He probably had a lot of experience hooking up in bars. He might not have thought she'd noticed when he warned off "Crazy" Jake, but she'd spotted Greg's action-hero stare. Too bad, she'd have to make it up to Jake another time. The two of them often exchanged ghostly stories when she finished work. Or rather, she listened while he rambled about the strange things he'd seen. He was a sweet man and it was a shame that so many people were willing to dismiss him just because his experiences didn't match theirs.

Speaking of ghosts, she had a ton of data to review from the night before. She'd have to go through all three camera feeds and listen to the audio recorder.

Jessica couldn't post the image from last night until she'd given her client a rundown of the activity she'd confirmed. She would have done it last night, only, she'd picked up a guy at the bar and brought him home.

She still couldn't quite believe that. It had been so out of character that it felt more like playing an undercover role than a memory. But she couldn't regret it.

Especially not when she wandered into her kitchen alcove and found the note propped on her counter.

I enjoyed last night and am really sorry I had to leave.

Give me a call. Let me make it up to you.

– Greg.

His number was scrawled across the bottom. Maybe she would give him a call. And maybe she should take some time out of her work for dating. If last night was any indication, she'd been missing out. She let her gaze wander over the dozens of images she'd captured. The hunt still thrilled her, even though she'd accepted long ago that most people equated her work with the ridiculous. Or worse, compared her to her mother.

She made herself some toast and grabbed fresh fruit from the fridge before settling in front of her computer. Making a face at the newsfeed headline—FBI MANHUNT FOR ESCAPED MILLIONAIRE CONTINUES—she clicked over to her email. People with money always think they're the exception. Her family had learned that lesson the hard way when her mother couldn't deliver everything her employer wanted. Aware of the incipient seethe building, she reminded herself it was all in the past.

Lesson learned, and she wasn't going to be caught in the same trap.

Luckily, her friend Paula needed a fact check on an article she was writing. A perfect distraction. Jessica loved reading Paula's articles, and this one promised to be especially good, about a rare variant of the Catholic exorcism rituals involving mirrors. She wanted Jessica's assistance on the details about different techniques using mirrors to aid in spiritual manifestations. Jessica sent it to the printer and turned to the message boards. Not a lot of activity, but she was pleased to see the overall number of hits was up on her site. Then she saw the new email blinking.

From: livlygrl@home.com
To: info@gotghosts.com
Subject: NEED HELP NOW!!!!
We need you to come right away! The situation is getting dangerous! It all started....

Jessica read the email, her concern growing by the minute. All thoughts of Greg faded away with the enticement of a new lure dangling before her.

"You did what?" Greg raged at his little sister. Petite and flamboyant, she had a metallic silver scarf wrapped around her Technicolor hair and wore a handmade black velvet bodice with dark gray lace. Cheap costume jewelry glinted a rainbow of fiery colors from multiple necklaces, chandelier earrings, and an enameled, heavy chain belt. She liked to call herself open-minded, but to Greg, it was all wishful thinking and gullibility. He needed to keep her from crossing the line into becoming some fraud's sucker.

"I called in a professional." Completely unaffected by his temper with the long-held practice of a baby sister, Olive held up two strands of bright blue hair against the brilliant sunlight streaming through the kitchen window, looking for split ends.

"I am a professional." Greg ground the words out through clenched teeth. He'd redone every inch of the kitchen for his parent's thirtieth wedding anniversary, putting in vintage cabinets and ceramic tiling. His work was not a hobby. If Olive thought she could hire someone else to do a better job—

"Not at this"—Olive dismissed him—"Hi, Mom."

"Hello, darling. Are you two fighting again?" Their mother had come in from the garden, dusting off her gloves.

"We're not fighting," Greg growled.

Tina Cooke raised an eyebrow at her errant offspring. Both of them looked away immediately. Satisfied with her display of parental power, she pulled off her gloves and began to wash her hands. "Are you staying for lunch, Olive?"

"No, I have to get back for class. I just wanted to let you know that I brought someone in to help with the situation." Olive handed her mother a brilliantly colored flyer.

Tina took it and her eyes widened in surprise. "Where did you find this?"

"At The Cauldron."

"What kind of contractor would advertise at The Cauldron?" Greg muttered under his breath. His sister practically lived at the alternative new age shop. No matter how unbelievably provoking Olive could be, he refused to devolve into a surly teenager. New age. If anyone asked him, the two words stuck together and rhymed with sewage. Excuses for flim-flam scammers to make a buck from dreamers. He caught a glimpse of the flyer and realized it was worse than he thought. He couldn't find the words he knew he needed to say. Shock froze his tongue.

"She'll be here at four," Olive told their mother, giving her a quick hug before dashing down the hall to the front door. They heard her car pull away a few moments later.

"You can't be—" he began, slamming the

flyer down.

"It won't do any harm," Tina cut him off wearily. "And to be honest, I'm not sure there isn't something more than leaky pipes and old wiring happening here." She patted his

shoulder the way she had when he was a child and upset over something. "You're good, Greg. One of the best. If it was mechanical, I'm sure you could have fixed it."

She reached for her gloves beside the sink, and her hand closed over empty tile. Greg turned and spotted them on a small table halfway down the long hall to the front of the house. A chill tried to wend its way down his neck and across his shoulders, but he resolutely shrugged it off. Olive probably moved them.

After his mother returned to her gardening, he glared at the flyer again.

GOT GHOSTS?
Strange noises? Things moving on their own?
Lights turning off and on by themselves?
YOU'VE GOT GHOSTS!
AND I CAN HELP!

He snorted in disbelief. How could anyone believe in this kind of crap? All day, Greg had been stewing over the potential conflict ahead this afternoon. When a battered truck pulled up in front of the house, he was ready to do ten rounds with the fraud who thought he could bilk his parents out of their hard-earned money.

He yanked open the door before the chimes of the doorbell died away. And stood there open-mouthed.

Jessica.

"What are you doing here?" he blurted.

"I got a call about a problem," she answered, clearly surprised. "Is this your house?"

"My... my parents' house." All the energy he'd prepared for the fight now cycled wildly through his body, cluttering up his brain and slowing his speech.

"That would be us, dear." Tina interjected herself between her son and their visitor. "I'm glad you could come."

"Me, too. Your daughter said it was fairly urgent?" Jessica sidestepped around Greg, letting his mother guide her down the hall to the kitchen. "How long have you been noticing strange things happening?"

"Almost two months now. At first, I thought I was getting old, misplacing my glasses or my book and such. Then things began disappearing out of drawers and reappearing in places they had no business being. Like my shoes showing up inside the oven." Tina shook her head to demonstrate her disbelief. "We began hearing strange noises, too. Banging and shuffling. Sometimes it sounds like someone walking around downstairs. Or like someone whispering in another room."

"It seems like a fairly typical progression for a manifestation," Jessica encouraged. She didn't even glance in Greg's direction.

He felt an immature urge to throw something or shout. Anything to get her attention. Less than twenty-four hours ago, she'd been gasping and shouting beneath him and now, she barely acknowledged him. The red imprints on his shoulders still ached. He didn't know what to think or how to process this sudden change. Something in his brain didn't want to lump her in with other scam artists, but he had to acknowledge to himself that he didn't really know her. She seemed like a good person, someone kind and interesting and compassionate. But she also apparently ran a business where she convinced people they had ghosts. His brain couldn't figure out which slot to put her in.

As she continued to listen to his mother, the surprise wore off, and he reminded himself that their personal history didn't matter. Greg wasn't going to let her convince his parents to waste their money on this nonsense. He'd debunk every damn stunt she tried to pull.

It took all of Jessica's long years of practice ignoring bullies to be able to keep her attention away from Greg and on the client while the older woman explained what had been happening in the house. She didn't need psychic powers to tell he was not a believer in the paranormal. She might have derailed him with surprise, but he was brooding his way back into a confrontation.

Jessica might not be the most sensitive person in her family, but something definitely haunted this house. The entire building was saturated in thick, oppressive atmosphere. The sunlight didn't quite touch inside despite the open windows. There was a presence here, and she'd bet all the equipment in her truck that it wasn't friendly.

Greg's mother showed signs of long-term exposure. Bags under her eyes from not sleeping well. Her skin was dry, and her fingers plucked and twitched constantly, both signs of severe and prolonged stress. Jessica's heart wanted to reach out and tell this woman that everything would be okay.

But she refused to make a promise she might not be able to keep. Still, it didn't mean she couldn't do anything to help. "It sounds like it's been difficult, Mrs. Cooke."

"Please, call me Tina. And it has."

"I'll be honest with you." Jessica spread her hands out on the table, knowing it would subconsciously reassure Tina. "People can tell you that old houses creak and moan. They can tell you that you or your husband should be tested for Alzheimer's, which can often start to show itself by finding objects in odd places. Those are rational and reasonable explanations for what's happening here, except I don't think that's what it is."

She took a deep breath to steady herself under Greg's antagonizing gaze. Even standing behind her, she could feel it like twin lasers burning into her back. "My family has a reputation for being sensitive, and when I walked in here, it was like the sun disappeared behind a cloud. You've probably been feeling it for weeks now."

Tina nodded, her foot tapping a nervous tattoo on the floor. "I hate coming in here when I've been outside in the garden. But it seemed so silly to be afraid."

"It isn't silly." Jessica reassured her client. They all needed to hear they weren't crazy for what they suspected. It was the first step in gaining their trust. "In fact, I'm going to suggest you and your husband spend a few nights at a hotel to get a break."

"And what will you do?" Greg growled.

Jessica ignored him but still answered the question. "I'm going to spend tonight documenting what happens in the house. Once I know what I'm dealing with, I can get some help to arrange for whatever is haunting you to move on."

"Like an exorcist?" Tina asked.

"I doubt we'll need one. Most of the times, hauntings are recordings of moments in time and can be gotten rid of with the energy equivalent of house cleaning." Jessica provided the simple answer even though her intuition warned her this would not be a simple situation. "A little salt, a little incense, and everything brightens right up."

"And how much for the salt and incense?" Greg butted in again.

"I don't charge for my services, Tina. The opportunity to document the spiritual world is why I do this." She couldn't resist turning in her chair to face Greg, capturing his gaze with her own. "In fact, I work two jobs to pay my expenses so I have time and the equipment to do this. I waitress at Billy's Breakfast Bar, and I answer the phones for the walk-in clinic. I know you think I'm a fraud and only out to make money, but I'm not."

She released him and he looked away. Her little trick hadn't done anything to assuage his anger and might only have made things worse. She was so damn tired of being judged.

Turning back to Tina, she asked, "Are you okay with letting me stay here while I do my work?"

"I am. And since this is still my house, it's my decision." Tina sent a warning look in her son's direction.

"I'm staying here, too. I don't want my folks coming back to find their house has been emptied." Greg issued his challenge with his muscular arms crossed over his broad chest. Jessica reminded herself not to get distracted by memories of the previous night. She had work to do.

Of course, work didn't stop her body from setting up a hum of approval along her nerves. Her libido didn't care if he was a judgmental ass. He was great in bed and it had been a long time. *Those talented fingers…*

Jessica mentally told her body to quit it with the color commentary.

"Fine with me. Just try not to disturb my equipment." She stood. "If it's all right with you, Tina, I'll do a walk-through and then set up."

The house would have been happy in other circumstances. Light, cheerful paint and wallpaper in shades of green and gold. Windows opened easily to the outside world rather than locking the occupants into an airless prison. Family pictures lined the slanting slope of the stair wall. She looked at a blond seven-year-old Greg proudly holding out a ribbon for some childhood contest, displaying a wide gap of missing teeth with his eager grin. The boy in the pictures grew older and the smile disappeared, replaced with the seriousness of a youth approaching manhood. She found herself missing the smile and told herself she was being ridiculous.

She tried to focus on her fingertips. Her mother and grandmother might have been able to see spiritual apparitions, but she only got tactile warnings—a strange sort of buzzing fullness that raised goosebumps on her skin in the presence of the paranormal. A quick brush of her fingers along the walls often told her the best places to put her equipment. Today, she couldn't be certain if the frisson sliding along her skin was because of a ghost or because of Greg.

That's what she got for letting herself walk on the wild side. In a regular dating scenario, she'd have figured out his prejudices pretty quickly, and this awkwardness wouldn't have come up. She'd have been protected, not left raw and vulnerable, having to share the house with a former lover who thought she was a fraud.

Watching his parents drive away, Greg cursed himself and his impetuousness. How did he end up in these kinds of messes, and why was he the only one who seemed concerned at leaving the house in the hands of a so-called ghost expert?

Jessica retrieved a heavy bag full of electronics from her car and had begun to place various cameras and other equipment around the house. He stared at one, a small box with a wavering needle.

"Please don't touch that," she said quietly behind him.

"What is it?" he demanded, feeling like a kid caught with his hand reaching for the cookie jar.

"An EMF meter. It detects changes in the electromagnetic field. Ghosts and other paranormal activity can cause alterations. So can humans, and if it's jarred or moved, its readings will be useless for a while," she explained. "I've set it up carefully so the infrared camera will see it."

He pointed at a squat box on the formal dining table. "What's that one?"

"A digital recorder. For EVP sessions."

Despite the crisp answer, she wouldn't quite meet his eyes.

"EVP?" He tried to keep his sarcasm level down below the Denis Leary threshold.

"Electronic voice phenomena. Sometimes you can hear voices on the recording that you couldn't hear by yourself." She left the room, tension clearly visible in her neck and shoulders.

Greg started to feel like a real jerk. He still didn't believe in any of this stuff, but she hadn't asked for money or balked at having him stay with her. She didn't seem to be playing an angle or running a con.

He caught up with her as she entered the kitchen. "I want to apologize."

She stared at him warily. "For last night or for calling me a fraud and a thief?"

"The second part. I didn't handle this well." He caught himself holding his breath, wondering how she would respond.

"I should be used to it." She relented, sitting down at the kitchen table. "Most people think what I do is crazy."

"Why do it then?" he asked.

"You don't believe in ghosts." It wasn't a question, just an opening.

"Nope. I think people like scary stories, and their imagination gets the better of them," he answered honestly.

She pulled a laptop out of a travelling case. "I do believe in ghosts. Which means I believe it's possible for people to become trapped between this world and the next one. I don't like the thought of people being trapped and scared, trying desperately to find someone, anyone who will be able to hear them and help them. Imagine shouting at the top of your lungs

36

and waving your arms and no one can see you or even knows you're there." She shuddered. "It's pretty much my definition of hell."

"It does sound awful," Greg acknowledged. He'd never thought about it from that perspective. Of how it would feel to be a ghost.

"That's why I do it. I want to help people, even dead people. I try and document everything I can. Someday, maybe we'll get proof, and then we can figure out what creates a ghost and how to prevent them." She began to plug her computer into the kitchen outlet.

Greg reached down to stop her. "Hold on. I've got a surge protector in my bag. The electrical has been going nuts in here. I've been trying to fix it but haven't had much luck."

"You're a contractor?" she asked. Greg rummaged and produced a multiple outlet surge protector with the required minimum six feet of cord. "I've always liked working with my hands, making things. I like taking something that's broken, or just plain trouble, and turning it into something that does what it's supposed to do."

Jessica carefully powered up the laptops and began plugging cords into them. She looked up at Greg, and her dimples made an abrupt appearance. "I suppose this is the kind of conversation we'd have had on our first date."

"I think it's going okay," he said, smiling back at her. No man could resist those dimples unless he was three-days dead. And from what she said, maybe not even then.

"We're managing to be civil, which is a step in the right direction." The screens burst into life, each showing a different camera angle of the house. One in the sitting room in front, another in the hall upstairs and a strangely colored one in the downstairs hallway.

"What's that one?" he asked, tapping the screen.

"It's a FLIR camera. It records heat. My newest baby." She smiled again. "Three months of tips for it, but it'll be worth it."

"What do you do now?" he asked.

"I'll monitor everything from here. Later, I might do a walkthrough or try an EVP session. I'm not sure yet." She bit her lip, and her arm crept up to wrap around her stomach.

A surge of protectiveness surprised him. "What's wrong?"

"This isn't a typical haunting. It's more. Darker." She tugged at her chin with her fingers, clearly struggling to explain in simple words. "Ordinarily, even in a strong manifestation, one where people are afraid… it doesn't feel like this. The air isn't thick and heavy, like someone breathing down the back of your neck."

Her words cast a chill over him, and he tried to break it with denial. "It's the humidity. These old houses hold the heat really well."

Irritation made the dimples vanish. "This

38

is more than airflow. You can't be so deep in denial that you can't feel it."

Time to jump back on the reality train. "I feel the stress my folks have been under for weeks. I feel how my mom bakes when she's upset and running the oven at all hours of the day has made this house stuffier than usual for this time of year. I feel how my dad has blocked a bunch of the vents downstairs with boxes and crates. There's barely room to move between them."

"Listen, you—" She stopped abruptly, her eyes fixed on the computer screen.

"What is it?" Greg asked, turning to look. Then he didn't have to ask.

An opaque dark figure, shaped like a human with an unusually broad head and long arms, had emerged from the master bedroom and was slowly walking toward the stairs.

"What the hell?!" Greg charged out of the room to confront the intruder.

"Greg! Wait!" Jessica called out after him, but he didn't hesitate. He was not about to let some burglar get away. He skidded along the hall, grabbing the corner post of the handrail to swing himself into position to run up the stairs.

Only… the stairs were empty. The burglar must have heard them coming. He pounded up the stairs and gasped in shock. Arctic cold slammed into his head and shoulders. The wintery chill stopped him with a physical impact. His chest was above the second level floor, but he couldn't force himself to take another step.

He heard Jessica coming up the stairs behind him. He saw his breath crystallize into a small cloud in front of him. A rattling sound filled the air.

"Not good," Jessica whispered, her eyes wide. The family pictures hanging on the walls were shaking, banging their frames in a rapid drumroll.

An earthquake? But this isn't anywhere near a fault line. It could be the burglar pounding on the wall to frighten them off, but he couldn't believe someone would have time to get out of sight. Not to mention that the pictures on both sides of the wall were active. Including the wall that only had the outside behind it.

Okay. Someone wants to pretend to be a ghost, I'll make him wish he was one! Greg shouted: "You think a little cold and some noise is going to frighten me off, Casper?"

"Greg, we have to get out of here." Jessica grabbed his arm and tried to pull him away. He shrugged her off easily. Bullies didn't impress him, either living or dead.

"Come on! That all you got?" he challenged.

The glass on the pictures shattered, flying toward them. Greg instinctively ducked, trying to cover Jessica's body with his own. He felt cold slices stinging along his back.

He picked her up and hauled her down

the stairs, shards of glass tinkling against the hardwood all around them. A low growl filled the house, like the roar of an ocean storm. The pictures downstairs were beginning to rattle against the walls.

"We can't stay!" Jessica shouted against the noise.

The front door swung open, and the two of them ran for it. Eerie, mocking laughter chased them out of the house. As their feet touched the front step, the door slammed shut, and they heard the tumblers clicking in the lock.

Greg tried the knob, but it didn't budge. The house was locked.

They slowly retreated down the front walkway. A muted roar still filled the air with bass, like the rumble from a loud movie next door. Lights flickered upstairs and on the main level.

"We have to leave. We need to get some distance between us and whatever is happening here," Jessica ordered, pulling him into her truck.

"What the hell is all this?" His feet jammed down on the invisible passenger gas, and his arm was braced against the oh-shit bar. In the driver's seat, Jessica spun the wheel, taking them away from his childhood home-turned-nightmare.

"I don't know, but right now it's too dangerous. We have to give things time to calm down." She looked over at him. "You're bleeding."

Once she mentioned it, he could feel wet splotches of blood on his shirt slapping coolly against his back. Jessica drove them to her apartment.

She cursed herself for getting involved, but she wasn't sure if it was about the house or being with Greg. They both frightened her with their intensity. She wondered what was happening with her equipment, not looking forward to a long spell of double shifts to earn enough for repairs and replacements. She'd discovered the hard way that insurance companies didn't cut any slack for ghostly interference.

For the second time in twenty-four hours, she found herself alone with Greg in her home. "Take off your shirt."

He stared at her as if she was propositioning him. Of course, it was true that people were supposed to be horny after dangerous situations. It explained the appeal of horror movies for date nights. But she had nobler intentions than riding him like a pony to relieve shock.

"I need to look at your back. Get the glass out. Make sure nothing needs stitches," she clarified.

He looked disappointed but pulled his shirt over his head. His magnificent back lived up to the half-glimpsed memories despite the angry slices marring the broad muscles.

She filled a bowl with cool water and then took some paper towels to start cleaning the cuts. Despite some bleeding freely, all of them were shallow. A few had already clotted over. She ran her fingers gently over the injuries, probing to see if any glass remained embedded in the skin. And trying very hard not to notice how warm and soft his skin was.

"What happened back there?" he asked quietly.

"Ghosts feed on strong emotions. My mother always said it was why they tried to frighten people, so they could use the energy to communicate. The more energy they can draw, the stronger the manifestation. When you charged up and challenged it, it could use the energy to attack us," she explained, only half of her mind on her words. The other half kept a tight rein on her libido.

"You really think it was a ghost back there." He sounded disappointed, as if she'd told him the tinfoil hat was to keep the CIA from reading her brainwaves.

She decided to fight logic with logic. "What do you think it was?"

He replied too quickly. "Special effect. Someone could have planted motors or something in the wall to make the pictures shake."

"You think it's more plausible to believe that someone broke into your house and seamlessly inserted something behind the drywall without leaving any trace behind? Why would someone do that?" She needed to make him start thinking about his assumptions if she ever wanted him to trust her.

He glared at her. "Maybe to get their name and face on TV."

Great. I'm back to being the culprit. "I've never been to your house before today, and I have no interest in being on TV. All those bastards care about are ratings." Jessica threw the bandages into her first aid kit with more oomph than was strictly necessary.

Greg held up his hands. "Okay, maybe that was a bad call."

"I know why people assume it's all fake." The anger drained out of her. "I see the clips edited for sensationalism, the outright fakes and frauds. Most of what's out there is garbage, because the real stuff isn't interesting enough to hold an audience's attention. People demand bigger and better and even the best-intentioned groups and people can find themselves caught up in the trap of enhancing rather than searching for the truth. It's one of the reasons I won't take money. I want to know what's really out there, rather than playing to what people want to hear."

His fingers wrapped around her hand.

"Okay. I can accept that. So, what do you think happened?"

"I think we saw a manifestation of a spirit, which succeeded in chasing us out of the house. What I don't understand is why." Jessica felt distressingly out of her depth.

"You don't think it was just trying to scare us? Build up the emotional energy or whatever?"

Jessica couldn't help but smile at the evidence he'd been paying attention. "It wanted us gone. Whatever is in the house has staked it out, like a wolf claiming territory. We're threats to it, but it can't follow us here."

"They can do that?" A slight note of panic entered his voice.

"A ghost can attach itself to a thing, a place, or a person. Sometimes it finds a person it likes better, and it will shift targets. But I have precautions against an attempt." She indicated the thick row of white crystals lying across the windowsill and beaded charms hanging on the walls and door. "Salt and charms prevent them from coming in here."

"It's hard to believe all this can be real," he said, sighing. "This morning, I knew anyone who believed in ghosts was either clinically insane or gullible."

"A hundred years ago, anyone talking about microbes would have been classified as crazy. Things change, and even if we want to believe otherwise, humans are barely beginning to grasp the world around them." Jessica smoothed the last bandage in place and dropped her hands into her lap to avoid touching him again.

"How did you get into this?" he asked. "My mother was a very famous medium. Lillian De Briand was her stage name." She hated talking about her mother, but questions were inevitable. It was best to get them out of the way early.

"She had a TV show," he said. "Something from the grave."

"*Spirit Sight: Conversations from the Grave*." Jessica's shrug was a little too deliberately casual. "She saw ghosts like you and I see each other right now. A lot of people tried to debunk her."

"There was a scandal. A plant from a newspaper, but she never picked up on it." Greg remembered the newspaper and magazine articles.

"She couldn't always make the connection, but there was a lot of pressure from the studio and her sponsors, so sometimes she'd just trust her intuition and make things up. That time, she got caught. She lost the show, we lost our house. She went back to private consultations. She'd bring me along to try and develop my gift. It didn't really work." She tried to avoid remembering the endless snapped accusations of lying and betrayal. Her mother never quite believed her when she explained she couldn't sense what her mother sensed. Not the latest scion of a long line of mediums and spiritualists.

"Sounds like it was tough. Why did you stick with it?" He took her hand in his.

"What happened to her pissed me off. The studio expected her to be on all the time, no holidays, no mistakes. The reporter expected her to be a total fraud. There was no understanding, no science she could rely on to explain what was happening. Why it sometimes worked and sometimes didn't. I might not be able to see what she saw, but I wanted to provide the science."

To her surprise, she saw understanding in his eyes. True believers accused her of undermining the art and mystery. Skeptics accused her of wasting time and money on garbage. No one had ever grasped the fine line she tried to walk between the two positions.

"That and helping people. Even dead ones," he replied, proving he got it. He leaned in and kissed her.

His mouth was warm and tasted sweet, like strawberry jam. Jessica exhaled and let herself relax into him. Her hands slid along the thick muscle of his arms, reveling in the smoothness. The man must wax more ruthlessly than anyone else she knew. There wasn't a solitary hair to mar the perfection of his body, except his dark eyebrows. The effect was well worth it.

She lay back, drawing him down over her.

He balanced easily, resting and rubbing along the length of her body without crushing her. After the fear earlier, having him surrounding her, enfolding her, protecting her— this was exactly what she needed.

His hand dipped inside her jeans to test her swollen folds while his tongue plundered her mouth. She felt his chuckle of masculine appreciation buzz against her lips.

Eager to continue, she broke the kiss so she could take off her shirt and began to twist to undo her bra. He helped, his deft fingers making easy work of the clasp.

"You don't have any pretensions," he whispered, running a hand over her bared chest.

"What you see is what you get," she agreed. "I like that." He bent to take one of her breasts in his mouth, softly rolling the nipple with his tongue. She might have been tempted to overanalyze the comment but for now, she was content to let it vanish beneath exquisite sensation.

Their wild coupling the night before had been all about passion and discovery. Now it was a reunion, taking the time to re-explore territory and find new aspects. How he growled in appreciation while worshipping her body with his mouth and hands. The way she shuddered and gasped when he brushed past a sensitive point. The play of shadows and candlelight over his muscles. His touch was gentle but thorough, until her mind was half-melted with pleasure.

When he entered her, they both clung to one another. He slid in and out, playing her body like a fine instrument. His control sent her past the first wave of orgasm into a blissful melody of ecstasy.

The house was quiet when they pulled up the next morning, like the calm after a hurricane. Greg unlocked the door, and they slipped inside. Glass glittered on the stairs in the morning sunlight and pictures hung askew on the wall, but otherwise, there weren't any signs of the disaster the night before. Greg pulled out his mother's vacuum and the broom, and the two of them began to clean up so they could move around safely. It took a while to dig all the tiny shards out of their hiding places, but eventually they got them.

Jessica went upstairs to check on her equipment. The infrared camera and the EMF meter were fine, but her new FLIR camera lay on the floor, the lens cracked. She cried out and Greg immediately came charging up the stairs.

"What the hell?" he demanded when no angry spirits were immediately apparent.

"It's broken. It'll take me months to save up for a new one." She gathered up the pieces to bring downstairs.

Greg didn't say anything, following close behind. She didn't quite know what to think about him. They'd shared two nights of great sex, true, but outside of the bedroom, he was a little too impatient and demanding—for her comfort level.

Luckily, the hard drives on the computers had recorded everything through the night. The dark shadow apparition, the rattling pictures, the flying glass. After the door slammed behind them, they could see various rooms lighting up in bursts and flashes. Doors opened and closed without any visible source.

The FLIR camera showed the lowered temperature in the upper hall when Greg came up. Everything went from purplish to deep blue in a matter of seconds, leaving Greg outlined in brilliant reds, yellows and whites. After the attack, the background gradually warmed again. Then it flashed deep blue once more as the camera was knocked to the ground and static replaced the image.

The material was too good. If she posted this, people would accuse her of hoaxing by having the doors and lights on remote openers, like on a movie set.

The EVP was the last thing on her list to go through. While Greg inspected the house, checking for damage and replacing burned out lightbulbs, she donned a pair of headphones and listened. Greg's shout and charge up the stairs were painfully loud, but she could still hear something underneath it.

She pulled up her audio enhancement software and carefully eliminated Greg's noise. Then she highlighted the tiny burst of sound remaining and listened to it over and over on repeat.

On the second listen, she caught her breath. A small child's voice cried out. "Don't go up there!"

The voice was staticky and so quiet that it was almost impossible to hear. But it was there.

She listened to the next segment and found another message. The front door clicked open and the voice said, "Hurry. He's mad."

"Greg!" she called out. He came down and she played the two segments for him, carefully not telling him what she heard. It was too easy to think you'd heard messages in the static that were actually only in your own head.

"It sounds like a kid telling me not to go up there." Greg's eyebrows threatened to sail right over his shaved pate. "Then he tells us to hurry."

"That's what I heard, too. It's the ghost haunting your parents." Jessica couldn't keep the triumphant grin off her face. This was something she could use. Something that made sense.

"You're telling me some kid did all this?" He frowned in disbelief.

"Kids can be the most dangerous spirits. Imagine a two-year-old throwing a tantrum and being able to grab everything off the walls with a thought."

He had clearly done some babysitting in his day because Greg winced at the image.

"We need to try another EVP session." Jessica grabbed the recorder.

Greg caught up to her in the living room. The overhead light began to flicker and blink, threatening to shut down.

"I know there's a spirit in this house." Jessica looked up at the fixture. "Blink the lights once for yes and twice for no. Would you like to talk to me?"

The light flickered once and then settled into steady illumination.

"Thank you," she replied. "I have a box here that will help us to hear you. Is that okay?"

Greg watched the light blink on and off again, no longer able to deny there was an intelligent entity controlling it. It amazed him how Jessica could be so fearless and confident while dealing with something so strange and unnatural.

She pressed rewind on the tape, then turned the volume up to listen. A clear, wavering voice came through immediately. "Can you see me?"

A child's simple and heartfelt plea. He wanted to believe she'd prerecorded it but couldn't force himself to challenge her.

"I can't see you. I'm sorry," she replied. "Can you tell me your name?"

Her lips moved in a silent count to ten. Then she rewound the tape.

"Tommy."

She looked up at him. "Do you know a Tommy? Does the name mean anything to you?"

"My best friend growing up was Tommy Lawrence. He and his wife are living happily four blocks away," he answered.

"That's not it then." Jessica chewed on her lower lip. "Whoever Tommy is, he's aware of us. Which means it can't be a residual haunting."

"A what?"

"A residual haunting. It's like an imprint from the past. An image or sound which repeats over and over without any awareness. Most of the time, it's not even the moment of death," she explained before turning her attention back to the ghost. "Tommy, have you always lived at this house?"

"Don't leave me," Tommy pleaded through the machine.

"I won't, sweetheart," she promised. "Have you always lived here?"

"Don't leave me with him!" Tommy wailed. The pictures began to rattle on the wall again and the temperature plummeted, raising goosebumps on both Greg and Jessica's bare arms.

She frowned. "Who? Greg? Greg won't hurt

you."

Greg saw a chair from the dining table jerk away from its place. Jessica faced the other way, oblivious to the chair grinding along the floor, picking up speed. The noise was disguised by the clattering pictures and knickknacks.

Jessica was still trying to connect with the child. "Tommy, you have to stop the noise or else I'm not going to be able to hear y—"

Greg didn't wait to think. He grabbed her by the waist and yanked her into the hall by the stairs. The chair slammed into the sofa, exactly where Jessica had been standing, with the bone-like crack of splintering wood.

Immediately the noise level dropped, leaving the house eerily quiet again. He could feel the quickened beat of her pulse under his hands. Her wide eyes left no doubt of her fear.

"You're telling me some kid did that?" he asked.

"I don't know," she replied, shakily holding up the EVP recorder. She rewound it, and the unbearably loud recorded sound of the animated furniture slammed into their ears.

Beneath it, a low growling snarled, "GET OUT!"

Greg opened his mouth to ask what the hell it was, but Jessica waved him to silence, concentrating on the EVP. A rush of air across the microphone marked where he'd grabbed her. Then silence fell before his blaring question about some kid doing this.

Tommy got the last word. "It wasn't me." "That wasn't a child." Jessica stared at the sleek little recorder. "It didn't even sound human."

"So, what was it then?" He demanded. If there had been any hair left on his neck, it would be rising.

"I don't know what they are. My mother warned me never to try and communicate with them. Some people say they're ghosts that are so old they've forgotten being human and have gone insane from the contact-deprivation. Others say they were never human at all." She returned to the kitchen and dragged a bag from under the table. The zipper rasped open under her impatient fingers, and she began to rummage through the contents.

Greg couldn't help but feel sunk well out of his depth. "What are you doing?"

"An exorcism."

"A what?" He couldn't possibly have heard what he thought he heard.

"An exorcism. I don't know what it was, but I'm getting it the hell out of this house." Her lips were compressed into a tight line.

He tried again. "Shouldn't you leave this to professionals? That thing sounded dangerous."

"A professional?" Shoulders squared, she finally lost her temper at him. "I am a professional. I've been doing this since I was a kid. I know what I'm doing. And I'm not going to leave a scared child trapped with that thing for one second longer than I have to."

This was the moment. He could continue to hold out doubts that this was all a delusion or some kind of trick, or he could accept that ghosts were real. If they were real, then she was right. A kid was trapped with some kind of monster. He couldn't walk away from it any more than he could walk away from a child being hauled into a kidnapper's van.

"What do we do?" he asked. She handed him a massive shaker full of white crystals while she used a lighter to ignite a thick braid of cedar and sweetgrass. When the braid began to smolder on one end, she motioned for him to follow her upstairs.

"Don't worry, Tommy. We'll take care of you and make sure he can't hurt you again," she called out, before focusing once more on Greg. "We'll start upstairs and work our way down, sealing each room against that thing."

She directed him to put down a thick layer of salt across each of the windows while she waved the smudge stick over the walls and

furniture, chanting the same words over and over. "Spirits, which would harm, begone. Only light and love may enter here."

She used the smoke like a broom, sweeping an invisible force into a smaller and smaller area before forcing it over the bedroom's threshold. Then she told Greg to seal the doorway with a line of salt. They repeated the process for each bedroom and then down the stairs, leaving the treads thickly carpeted with white.

Next, she cleared the sitting room, then the hall, and finally the kitchen, pushing whatever she was fighting over the back door and onto the porch. When she slammed the door shut, the air seemed cleaner and brighter. Greg held on tight to his half-full container. He'd expected more in the way of bells and whistles and special effects. "Is that it?"

"That's it. It's not perfect since whatever it is will still be out there, but it won't be able to come back in. Not without an invitation."

Jessica carefully placed the smudge stick in a saucer to let it finish burning. "There are people I can call who will help with that part. Now we have to make sure Tommy is okay."

She looked up at the kitchen lights.

"Tommy, if you're still here, make the lights blink once."

The lights obediently turned themselves on and then off. She pulled out the EVP recorder. "I'm glad you're all right, Tommy."

"Is it safe now?" The frightened voice returned on the recording.

"It's safe now. Everything is all right," she smiled. Then her eyes went wide.

"What is it?" Greg whirled around but there was nothing in the empty hall.

"I can see him," she whispered. "A little boy,

about seven years old. Blond hair. He's wearing a *Superfriends* T-shirt and bell-bottom jeans. He's right there."

She knelt, holding out the EVP recorder like a lifeline. "Tommy, do you want to stay here?"

"I like Tina and Bill. They're nice. They miss their kids," the recorder answered.

"Wouldn't you like to be with your mommy and daddy?" she asked.

Greg wished he could see what she saw.

"No," said Tommy. "They went away and never came back. I miss Grandma. She was nice." His voice was clearer, less like popping static. "She went to the light."

"Would you like to go to the light?" Jessica asked.

"What about Tina and Bill? Who'll take care of them?" Tommy replied.

"I'll take care of them, kid. Don't worry," Greg answered gruffly.

"He's smiling at you," Jessica whispered, her beautiful face glowing with compassion and interest. She held out her arms and then folded them gently around something. For a moment, he couldn't figure out what she was doing, but then he grasped it. A hug.

A hug for a little boy who'd been forgotten for forty years.

As he stared, he could see a change in the air in Jessica's embrace. It was brighter, like someone shining a flashlight through wisps of fog. Then it vanished. He saw a tear glittering on Jessica's cheek.

"He's gone now," she told him. "I've never been able to see them before. And now he's gone."

Greg pulled her into his arms, holding her tight. He might have wanted her when he first saw her in the bar but now, seeing her bravery and compassion, he knew he was treading into dangerous territory. But for the moment, he didn't care.

"He tried to say something at the end." Jessica laid her head on his chest as she examined the recorder. With expert precision, she rewound and played the recording.

"Watch out for the Bad Thing in the basement."

Tommy's final warning chilled the afterglow.

"You have a basement?" Jessica stepped out of his embrace, her voice flattened with worry.

"Um. Yeah. It's where my dad keeps his stuff and his tools for work." Greg rubbed the back of his neck, feeling the goosebumps rising again.

"What kind of work?" Her eyes and lips narrowed.

"He buys antiques and stuff from estate sales and fixes them up." Greg kept talking to avoid the inevitable explosion. "It's pretty full right now. He got a heck of deal on the contents of this one old lady's house. She'd been hoarding for years, never left the property. Her relatives didn't want to deal with it, so Dad got it for a steal."

"When was this?" she demanded.

"About four months ago. It took him almost a month to go through and sort the junk from the useful stuff. He told me about all the weird things she owned, a stuffed cat with two heads, magazines from the thirties, a demon box—" Greg began to warm up when Jessica cut him off.

"A demon box?"

"Yeah. A little cabinet sealed with wax. Dad thought it might make a great bedside table, so he sanded it down and refinished it." Jessica began to walk away while Greg was still talking. "What's the big deal?"

"First off, I didn't know about the basement, so we didn't seal and purify it, which means whatever was haunting this place is probably still down there. Second, you never told me your dad opened up a demon box right before all the problems started?" she snapped at him.

"Wait, it's not like any of it was real," Greg snapped back, irritated.

"After what you've just seen, you can really say that?" Jessica looked around the kitchen. "Where's the door?"

"In the back corner, on the far side of the

fridge," he replied. "Okay, I'll admit to losing some skepticism when it comes to ghosts—but demons? Come on. You said it yourself; kids' spirits can throw some real tantrums."

Jessica yanked on the basement door. The knob wouldn't turn in her hand, and the door wasn't moving. There was no time to waste. Her mind whirled with the need to contain whatever it was. Should she call in reinforcements? Would salt and willpower be enough to contain a demon until help arrived? All of her efforts to open the door proved useless. *Maybe Greg has some ideas.* She turned to ask.

The door flew open behind her, knocking her forward into him. He automatically steadied her, bracing her with his forearms.

She felt something wrap itself around her waist, like a greasy invisible tentacle. Before she could say anything, it pulled her backwards. Her fingers scraped down Greg's arms as she hurtled through the gaping door.

She caught a glimpse of Greg's shocked and anguished face before she plummeted.

Then the door slammed itself closed.

Greg pounded on the door hard enough to make the walls rattle, shouting Jessica's name. The door refused to move for him.

He couldn't hear anything downstairs. Were her screams for help being muffled somehow? Or had she hit her head on the way down, knocking herself unconscious? He wouldn't even let himself think of worse options. Panic lent strength and speed to his blows. The door warped under his strikes but wouldn't open.

"All right, you want to play rough? You messed with the wrong freakin' contractor," he growled. His bag of tools was still in the kitchen.

His prybar was still in his car, and he didn't want to leave the house long enough to go get it. His favorite heavy duty flat-head screwdriver was instantly drafted into active service. He wasn't about to waste time unscrewing the hinges. Instead, he jammed the screwdriver head into the wood behind the hinges and used a heavy mallet to drive it in like a wedge.

The upper hinges came out easily and the distracted analytical part of his mind made a note to check the frame for dry rot later. A few more blows and the lower hinges clattered to the linoleum.

Despite all the laws of construction and gravity, the door still stood.

Hefting the mallet like a club, Greg smashed it into the wood with all the strength of twenty years of continuous heavy lifting.

Caught between arcane power and muscle power, the door took the only option it had left.

It broke into a half dozen shattered pieces.

Greg charged down the fragile basement stairs. Bouncing off the side of the landing, he leapt over the final few steps before skidding to a halt.

Stuffed with odd ends of furniture and boxes and lit with an eerie red light, the basement looked like some kind of survival shelter. The kind from movies where everyone is trapped inside and discovers the shelter isn't the sanctuary they expected. He couldn't see any movement.

"Jessica!" he shouted. The thick airswallowed his cry a few feet from his mouth. He tried again, bellowing. "Jessica!"

"Greg!" a muffled reply came from the right. His dad's workbench.

He ran around a stack of boxes and saw her sitting on a wooden chair. One his dad had been working on.

"Greg, be careful, it's—" Her words choked off into incoherence, and her shoulders jerked spasmodically. As if she were struggling to break free of ropes that tied her arms to the chair's arms.

Only, there weren't any ropes visible. A frisson of fear attempted to ice over his spine, but Greg was too pissed off to let it.

Jessica lifted her head, her big brown eyes wide with fear.

He spotted the small cabinet sitting on one

side of the workbench, its dark finish gleaming in the sullen light. He raised the mallet to smash it.

Jessica's muffled shout stopped him. Arms still raised and tensed, he looked back at her.

She was shaking her head vigorously. "Go ahead. Do it," a harsh sibilant whisper slithered through the air.

Jessica shook her head even harder. Greg lowered the mallet. He might be new to the world of ghosts and demons, but he'd seen enough horror movies to know that if the evil thing is encouraging you to do something, then doing it would not be good.

"Who are you?" he demanded.

"Asking my name? A refreshingly direct approach." The unseen spirit chuckled.

"Let Jessica go," Greg ordered.

"No"—it laughed—"I'm starved for company and conversation."

This thing unnerved him. It seemed to circle him, examining him for weaknesses. "Kidnapping people isn't a great way to get invitations."

"She started it. Trying to kick me out without even a hello," it replied maliciously.

"Let her go." He wished the darn thing had eyes or a face he could glare down. It was hard to deal with something he couldn't see.

"Power runs in her blood." The shadows around Jessica's face deepened and her body twitched as if flinching from something touching her. "She'll be the perfect vessel."

Vessel did not sound good. Greg impulsively reached out to grab one of Jessica's arms, hoping to snatch her from the seat and away from the Bad Thing's influence.

When his fingers touched the darkness, he felt a searing, knifing pain. He'd once plunged his hand into ice-water after a dropped tool, and that had been pleasant compared to this.

Despite his mental determination, his physical body reneged and yanked his hand back.

The fingers were white and slightly shriveled, as if frostbitten.

"Ah-ah. Mustn't touch." The Bad Thing's voice filled with glee. "You do care for her, don't you? It's strong. Stronger than I thought."

Greg was fairly certain he would not be happy when the thing's train of thought reached a conclusion.

He was right. "She's proving resistant to me. But I suspect that if I break you, she'll respond nicely."

Tears spilled down Jessica's face. She struggled harder to free herself.

"It's already working," it said with a chuckle. "If she responds so strongly to words, imagine how she'll be when I braid a rug from strips of your skin."

The mental image was enough to summon a

gagging ball of bile into the back of his throat. But it was nothing compared to the idea of watching Jessica break while she watched him being tortured.

"Of course, there is an alternative," it offered.

"What?" Greg couldn't take his eyes off Jessica. There must be a way to protect her.

"If you offered yourself to host me, I would let her go," the creature promised.

"Let her go first. Then you can have me." Greg didn't even have to think about it.

Jessica's incoherent denial abruptly transformed into words. "Can't! No!" She rushed toward him, knocking the chair aside.

"Run!" Icy tentacles wrapped around Greg's skin. He didn't trust this thing to keep its word.

"Greg!" she cried out, the anguish in her eyes clear. *She needs to get away from this house.* He felt the demon prying at his closed mouth. He had to make her see.

"Go!" he shouted before the demon's essence slid inside him like icy liquid, burning his throat with cold.

Jessica could see the exact moment Greg's personality vanished beneath the demon's. His warm blue eyes iced over, becoming cold and

66

distant.

His hand shot out and grabbed her arm in a bone-crushing grip. "You should have listened.

I only promised to let you go. Not let you escape."

"You can't have him!" she snarled back, her mind frantically reviewing every lesson her grandmother and mother ever taught her. There had to be something useful.

"I have what I want now. A physical body makes violence so much easier. And you got rid of the infuriatingly helpful little Tommy. There's nothing to stop me." It held her with both hands now, and she could feel bruises forming. Although it held Greg's body, there was nothing of Greg left in it, making it easy for her to see the demon instead.

Jessica's head swung back and forth, searching for anything she could use against the demon. The empty demon box squatted on the workbench. There must be a way to get the Bad Thing back inside.

"Interested in my little prison?" It released her with one hand, using Greg's body to open up the small cabinet, revealing a tiny space

barely large enough to hold a paperback or two. "I lived in there for decades. Should we try to see if you'd fit?"

I don't have any tools for an exorcism. She frantically scanned the workbench and spotted two mirrors leaning against a stack of furniture.

Paula's article! Except she still didn't have the proper tools, especially not for a full Latin-directed ritual. But do I really need any of that? Her mother and grandmother had insisted that a trained will was enough to contain any spiritual manifestation. The tools didn't possess any particular powers except for through the belief of their users. If she could only get the demon out of Greg, perhaps she could force it back.

She twisted her arm, breaking the creature's grip. Once she was free, she stepped backwards, moving closer to the old mirrors. They must have been part of a boudoir because they were massive and set in a movable wooden frame. Hopefully Paula's sources were right about mirrors and incorporeal spirits.

The demon opened and closed Greg's fingers, examining the hand closely. If it really had been trapped for decades, it might not know about martial art techniques.

"You really think you're frightening me?" she said, sneering.

Its eyes narrowed. Good. She'd struck a nerve.

"You're nothing but talk," she continued. "Rattling a few pictures, breaking a little glass. Please, I've seen scarier things waiting in line at Disneyworld."

A puzzled frown. Damn, I lost it on the reference. She had to break it down. This thing wanted fear. Scorn would undermine it.

"And now you're trapped in a nonbeliever. Smooth move." She forced her face into a mocking smile.

It snarled, moving closer. Jessica took a step back, closer to the mirrors.

"Your attempt at bravado has ceased to amuse." It flexed Greg's arms and shoulders. "This body might be a nonbeliever, but it will do nicely for what I have in mind. You found it attractive enough; luring others will be easy."

"Whatever." She rolled her eyes, assuming a pose of bored contempt.

As she suspected, it was too much for the creature's fragile ego. Hissing, it launched itself at her.

She fell backwards but managed to yank a mirror out of its place. She held up the massive piece with the glass facing her attacker.

It froze, muscles twitching.

"Fight it, Greg!" she shouted. "Drive it out!"

His hands opened and closed in fists, muscles jumped in his neck and chest. Rapidly conflicting emotions struggled to dominate his face, flashing from rage to concern to hatred to pride.

She held the mirror steady, using it to keep the demon in place. There wasn't any room to run in the narrow corridor between piles of junk and the workbench. Its only method of escape would be to flee Greg's body and hope she couldn't recapture it.

It was going to charge her, to try and knock the mirror aside. They were too close to each other. If he struck true, he would knock the glass from her grip. Jessica tightened her fingers until they went white.

The Bad Thing bellowed and lunged forward, arms flailing. She barely dodged the blow. Her muscles screamed with the effort of holding the heavy glass in place, but she held it focused squarely on the creature.

"Get. Out." Each word bit off with all the force of her will behind it.

"Willing host!" Greg's features twisted nearly to unrecognizability.

"You threatened to kill me. That's coercion and that undermines your hold. I know he's fighting you! Get out!" There would be no negotiation. Although if she'd allowed herself to waver, the demon could take advantage of her uncertainty. It would have tricked her too. But centuries of dealing with noncorporeal beings ran in her veins and in her mind. It had no choice.

Slowly, shadows began to trickle out of Greg's mouth and nose. The Bad Thing coalesced, glaring at her with the promise of painful slow death.

Greg collapsed to the concrete, rasping painfully as he tried to refill his lungs.

The demon swelled larger and larger.

Jessica's already dry mouth became desiccated. If it broke the confines of the mirror, it might still escape. And she wouldn't catch it again with the same trick.

"Greg!" she shouted.

He rolled onto his hands and knees, still coughing. "Get the other mirror."

He didn't question, just grabbed the heavy piece still resting in place.

"Hold it on it!" she ordered. He complied and she shifted so the two of them were bracketing the creature.

"Step forward!" He matched her step for step. The two of them drove the Bad Thing back toward its box. It snarled and spit at them like a furious cat, promising untold tortures once it broke free.

"In the box." She commanded it with her best disappointed-parent voice.

It slunk inside, still struggling to find an opening. Once the last of the greasy shadow reluctantly crossed into the small storage cavity, Jessica dropped her mirror in a resounding shatter of glass and wood.

She slammed the two doors shut on the demon box, throwing her weight on top of it.

"We have to seal it," she shouted at Greg. Now despair threatened. She didn't have any prepared candles to melt to seal the box or salt to make a protective circle. The demon was already rattling the doors hard enough to make her jump and shift.

If Greg ran upstairs to get her bag, could she hold the box closed long enough for him to make it back? She gritted her teeth, preparing to tell him to run.

A rasping ripping sound caught her attention. Greg bent close to her, shoving something silvery across the wood. She stared at it, her brain too numb to recognize it initially.

Duct tape.

Ordinary, industrial duct tape.

And it was working. With each plastic length wrapped around the box, the noise of the demon inside was muffled. Greg wrapped it like a mummy, leaving no square inch of wood uncovered. And when he finished, he began to wrap it in strands going the other way.

He unloaded two full rolls of tape onto the demon box. When he finished, the box sat quietly in place like any inanimate object.

"First rule of construction. You can fix any problem with enough duct tape," he choked out the words.

"It's working. I can't sense the demon anymore." Jessica shook her head. "But in case I'm wrong…" Getting into the spirit, she grabbed a Sharpie from the workbench and drew an elaborate set of protective symbols over the silver tape. When she finished, she shoved the entire thing into an industrial garbage bag. Greg used a third roll of tape to seal it.

"Now what?" he asked.

"I'll take it somewhere and bury it in consecrated ground. That should keep it contained." Jessica accepted the bulky package. "Do you want to go to the hospital?"

"I don't think my insurance covers demon-attacks. I don't care what you do, just get that thing out of the house." Greg shook his head. "This is too much weird shit for me."

Jessica nodded, hearing what he didn't say. He hadn't wanted to be a believer in the first place, and now he'd been forced to see something that made her, an experienced ghost hunter, want to curl up and forget she'd ever heard about the paranormal.

He stumbled up the stairs, not looking back. She heard him collapse on the couch while she gathered up her equipment. When she peeked into the living room, she saw he was sound asleep. Quietly, she withdrew. She'd call his parents once she got everything into the truck. Someone would be with him while he struggled to forget what happened to him. Including her.

"How would you like your eggs, sir?" Jessica kept a bright smile on her face despite feeling like she needed a shower after each leering glance from the guys at tables four and seven. What was it about waitresses that made men feel the need to ogle? Was it the combination of friendliness, bringing food, and short skirts? If it was this bad serving eggs and bacon to truckers and early morning commuters, she didn't want to imagine what it would be like in a bar.

She'd worked double shifts for the last two weeks, trying to earn enough to replace her FLIR camera. And, if she was honest with herself, to try and avoid thinking about Greg and the demon box. The whole experience still unsettled her. She'd posted her EVP conversation with Tommy and the online ghost hunting community had exploded over it. Some accused her of hoaxing while others demanded she tell them where the encounter took place so they could go talk to him, too.

Thank God, Tommy was beyond their reach now. A poor confused little boy didn't needpeople poking at him and demanding he perform like some kind of trained animal. Hopefully he was with his Grandma, happy and whole again.

She'd received a grateful email from Greg's parents and his sister, telling her there was no more activity in their house. She was almost finished her report for them. It would be completed once she could decide whether or not to tell them about the Bad Thing in the basement. Greg wouldn't want his parents to know what happened to him, but her conscience insisted they deserved the whole story so they could protect themselves in the future. *This is the reason I shouldn't get involved with clients*, she told herself. The truth shouldn't be held hostage. Even still, she couldn't bring herself to do it.

Everything about this case had turned into a snarled mess. She retreated to the washroom, afraid she might cry from the sheer exhaustion of riding constant emotional turmoil. She wanted to call Greg, but at the same time, she didn't want to hear him reject her. She wanted to explore her new sensitivity to the paranormal, but was afraid she would get overwhelmed like her mother. She felt like everyone was barking at her, demanding something, and if she didn't retreat, she would lose everything and be nibbled to death.

She splashed cold water on her face, reminding herself to take it one day at a time. Unlike most people who saw visions or heard voices, she had a reason for what she saw and heard. She was in a position to do more than she'd ever hoped. If only it didn't feel so empty and anticlimactic.

"Hey, Jessica," Sally said, poking her head into the washroom. "You've got a new customer in your section."

"I'll be out in a minute." She dried her face

and composed herself, setting her features into a bright and friendly smile. She needed the tips.

When she rounded the corner and saw the table, all speech vanished from her lips.

Greg sat at the tiny booth, his six-foot-plus frame looking ridiculously squished. He saw her and grinned. "I heard this place is pretty good. What do you recommend?"

"The carnivore plate isn't bad," she replied automatically before demanding, "What are you doing here?"

"Paying down a debt." He pulled a bag from the seat beside him and unwrapped the plastic to reveal a brand-new FLIR camera.

"You didn't have to do that," she replied. Her heart sank with inexplicable disappointment.

"It wasn't the only reason I came." He rose up out of the booth and brushed his hand along her cheek. "I was hoping I wasn't too late."

"Too late for what, exactly?" She told herself she was going to maintain composure.

"For this." He bent and took her lips in a flame-seared kiss.

For the last two weeks, she'd tried to convince herself that her memory had glossed over the flaws in his performance. No one could have actually been that skilled. But when his mouth touched hers, she knew she'd been lying to herself. Every line of her body thrilled to his touch, flaring into sensual excitement.

He released her long before she was ready to go. She found herself staring at his mouth, trying to suppress every memory of how talented he was with it.

"I thought you didn't want to see me again." She forced the words out. If he was going to leave, she wanted the Band-Aid ripped off cleanly and quickly. She couldn't survive a lingering break.

"You can't hold a guy's post-possession words against him," he teased, running his thumbs over her shoulders. "I got overwhelmed and needed space, but I didn't want you to disappear."

"Hold on." She held up a hand to stop him from kissing her again. If there was going to be any hope of this, she couldn't let him turn her brain to pudding with kisses. "What are you saying?"

"I'm saying this is too good to let you walk away. I don't know where it's going, but I know I want to find out." He studied her. "How about you?"

"I can't walk away from what I do," she warned him.

"Not asking you to. Not much call for this otherwise." He tapped the camera in its box. "Just tell me, do you deal with demons every week?"

She couldn't help laughing at the nonchalant question even as she shook her head. "No."

"Then we're good. Come on, you can use someone who can point out creaky stairs and drafty window fittings. No sense wasting your talent on things with an ordinary explanation." He cupped her face, stroking her hairline with the tips of his fingers. "I thought maybe we could call ourselves *Spirit Sight*, after your mom's show. A little bit of vindication for her."

"We? You want to be my partner?" Please say yes.

He nodded. "Damn straight. What do you say? Are you in?"

"I'm in." She pulled him in and nodded against his forehead. He captured her mouth again, sending her heart racing and her toes curling.

"Great, because the first thing we need to talk about are those flyers…"

Rose on the Grave

#2 Spirit Sight

Greg slid out of bed quietly, careful not to disturb Jessica. Even after two months together, he still wore a goofy smile whenever he saw her or thought about her or heard anything that reminded him of her. His sub-contractors had noticed his tendency to dissolve into broad smiles without warning and razzed him mercilessly about it. He didn't care though. *Let them laugh. I got the real prize.*

He padded barefoot across the cool hardwood floor to the bathroom, noting a few rough patches and deep scratches. Maybe he could arrange to refinish the floors for Christmas. He'd need to find an excuse to get her out of the apartment for a few days.

Closing the bathroom door so the light wouldn't leak out and wake Jessica, his heart began to thud in his chest once the door latched. He started hyperventilating and grew dizzy from lack of oxygen. *Don't be silly*, he scolded himself. *You're way too old to be scared of the dark.* Even so, he didn't waste any time flicking on the light.

Only to find himself facing a nightmare in

the mirror. Instead of his reflection, a demonic visage of fangs and shadows snarled a smile at him.

"Surprise!" it hissed in sibilant triumph. Greg couldn't move; the entity had locked his muscles in place. It grinned even wider and began to seep out of the mirror towards him. Greg struggled to run, to shout and warn Jessica, to do anything, but instead he could only stand helplessly when the first icy tentacles caressed his face.

He sat up, bellowing and flailing his arms. His legs were trapped, and he kicked hard, trying to break free of the creature's grip.

Something grabbed his shoulder, and he lashed out with strength built from over a decade of construction and demolition. He heard Jessica cry out and he struggled even harder, determined to reach her before the creature could.

His brain struggled to make sense of what his eyes were telling him. He didn't see the fixtures in the bathroom. Instead, gauzy and patterned swatches of fabric fluttered in front of his face. As if he were still in the bedroom.

The sleep-fog suddenly cleared, blown away by sudden panic. "Jessica!"

"I'm here." She slowly appeared over the edge of the bed, pushing herself upright. Sleep-rumpled, blond hair hid her face from him, but he could see her hand cupping the side of her face. Shock slapped him. She must have tried to wake him, and he'd struck out at her.

"Let me see," He reached for her, but she avoided him, padding barefoot to the kitchen in her oversized Casper T-shirt and a pair of his boxers. Usually the sight of her in his clothes was an immediate turn-on, but his actions had put an icepack on any arousal.

"It's fine. Probably won't even leave a mark." She opened the tiny freezer and dropped some ice into a plastic bag before wrapping a towel around it. She covered her reddened cheek and swollen eye, the injuries belying her reassurance and leaving Greg to simmer in his guilt.

He ran his hands over his scalp, resting his elbows on his updrawn knees and trying to get his pounding heart back under control. *Show's over, adrenaline. Just a drill. Nothing to worry about.* Except the increasingly frequent nightmares.

He couldn't even talk to anyone about it except Jessica. If he told a shrink that he'd been briefly possessed by a demon and worried about it coming back, they'd lock him up so fast, he'd never get back out. And he wasn't about to share his feelings with the guys on his crew. He'd be up to his knees in fake ghosts and bad practical jokes.

Jessica kept reassuring him the entity from the demon box was contained, and she'd taken it to a professional exorcist. He believed her

83

but couldn't keep from worrying it might get free someday. He'd had the damn thing in his head and knew if it ever got loose, it would come after the two of them for revenge. He'd wrapped the box in duct tape to seal it shut, but he would have much rather encased it in concrete or something else more solid. Something that could guarantee it was never coming back.

"Nightmares again?" The mattress dipped under Jessica's weight. Greg didn't trust himself to look at her, much less ever touch her again.

"I'm sorry," he whispered. Only scum hit women, so what did that make him?

"It was an accident. I shouldn't have touched you until you were awake." She wrapped her arm around him and laid her uninjured cheek on his shoulder. "Want to talk about it?"

The cool downdraft from the ice licked at his bare skin, ensuring he couldn't pretend this was a normal night for the two of them. Lacing his fingers together, he stared at them as if the world's fate depended on the steadiness of his gaze. Jessica's understanding only made him feel worse. The memory of the redness and swelling around her eye spoke the necessary accusations clearly enough.

"I'm sure it looks worse than it is." Jessica's attempt to make him feel better only deepened the guilt.

"It looks like someone should haul my ass to jail for abuse."

"Hey, we both have had nightmares about what happened. It's only natural."

True, but Jessica never lashed out during her bad dreams. She curled into a tight ball and whimpered soft cries that tore apart his heart. He pulled away from her, standing up. "We should both try and get some more sleep."

The clock's glow revealed another two hours before they needed to get up—Jessica for her waitressing shift at Billy's Breakfast Bar and Greg to supervise the installation of his client's new kitchen cabinets.

"I won't be able to sleep if I'm worried about you brooding in the bathroom," Jessica pointed out. "Come and lie down."

He let her coax him onto the mattress, but he held his distance. "Maybe I should stay with my folks for the next few nights."

A year ago, he'd been on track to a "normal" life, living with a doctor and planning to become engaged at some point. He'd scoffed at his sister's beliefs in ghosts, magic, and people with strange powers. Now his ex-girlfriend,

Janet, was engaged to some big investment banker who shared her love of exotic travel while Greg balanced his nights between bunking at his parents' home and staying with

Jessica. And he'd seen enough to know his sister Olive wasn't entirely wrong, although he still couldn't understand how she could believe in a shape-shifting video on the Internet was real. He might accept ghosts as real now, but a woman turning into a bear defied physics. It wasn't even a clever fake, with the woman disappearing behind a chair, then the bear appeared on the other side.

"I'd rather you were here." Jessica's cool hand smoothed the knotted muscles in his back. She cuddled up against him, her warm breath caressing the nape of his neck. He cursed himself for being weak, but he cupped her hand in his, holding it against his heart.

"I won't push you if you don't want to talk," she whispered, kissing his neck. "But I'm here for you." She sighed against him, her lithe body relaxing into sleep.

Tenderness melted his scoffing train of thought. When he'd been with Janet, he'd never wanted to hold her through the night. He preferred having his space on his side of the bed. He'd always thought it was the best part of their relationship—not being clingy like so many other couples. Janet had her own life and interests and he had his; they didn't need the other to validate or tag along. Even when Janet complained she felt disconnected from him, he'd assumed it was only a matter of tweaking the ratios of together-time versus separateness. Like setting up an HVAC system for the perfect balance between the furnace and air conditioning.

Now he found himself resenting every moment he and Jessica spent apart. He'd call or text her from work, and she did the same.

Luckily, the manager at Billy's was a romantic at heart who didn't mind the distraction, provided Jessica didn't drop orders or leave customers waiting. To his surprise, Greg even enjoyed going with her on paranormal investigations, and spending the night in a haunted house hadn't been on his Top 100 list even before he believed it was more than hokum.

Lately he'd noticed she was tenser during the investigations. They'd finish a night of recording and observing, and Jessica would be close to tears during the drive home. He'd thought they might be leftover fears, like his own. With the relationship so fragile, he didn't want to push. But after the last time, he could no longer ignore it.

Last weekend, they'd driven seven hours to investigate a home where the family was seeing dark shadows on the wall and hearing voices in the night. After spending another eight hours documenting, they had some fuzzy electronic voice phenomena and some odd movements of shadows that didn't correspond with the lights outside. It seemed like a fairly good investigation to him, but Jessica seemed depressed, barely speaking to him over breakfast. She was a pale echo of herself, like the first coat of paint on fresh drywall. The color had faded out of her.

On the car ride home, she'd finally told him. "It's not working anymore."

Oh shit. Had he forgotten her birthday? Or was this because he'd dropped the beer on top of the eggs in the grocery cart?

She must have seen the fear and humiliation starting to break the scale because she quickly shook her head, her teeth denting her lush lower lip. "It's not like that. I'm just not seeing what I need to."

Pulling down her baseball cap lower over her face, she hunched down in the seat and stared out the window.

"Okay, I think you're going to need to explain this for the studio audience. Or else." He imitated his father at his most serious.

"Or else what?" She straightened up, brown eyes wide in surprise.

"Or else I start singing Johnny Cash. Badly." Her lips started to twitch and much-needed laughter rang out. The broken yellow lines on the road dashed past them like some sort of code as the sun rose higher into the sky.

"Come on, take pity on me. I'm a big clueless contractor. I need it all spelled out in little letters with the dots drawn real close together." He let go of the steering wheel with his right hand to caress her thigh.

"I can't sense anything," she blurted, her cheeks stained with pink.

He frowned, slowing down the truck and preparing to pull over. "What do you mean?"

"I mean I can't sense anything at the sites. I can't see the ghosts, and I can't hear them except on the EVP." The words spilled out of Jessica like dirt from a cracked foundation wall. "After what happened with Tommy and the box, I thought I was finally becoming a medium like my mother and grandmother. But it's all gone."

He parked on the shoulder, giving her his full attention. Big rig trucks whizzed by in great rushes of air, rocking their truck on its tires.

"I couldn't see anything at the last house. I couldn't hear anything." Tears darkened her long lashes.

His first instinct was to fix the solution, to say anything to make her feel better. "Maybe there wasn't really a ghost there."

"You heard the EVP."

He'd heard something that might have been a voice in the static but nothing like the clear communication they'd received from Tommy, the child-ghost haunting his parents' home. They'd captured two possible messages last night, one sounded like "Call the doctor" and the other might have been "Time for a story," but neither were distinct enough to say for sure. "You're the one who told me humans look for patterns so hard they somet imes find them when they aren't there. Especially for voices and faces."

Most of her explanation went over his head, but if he'd gotten the gist right, humans were programmed to be aware of other humans and predators. So, they were quick to see faces in inanimate objects like electrical sockets and to hear voices in random noise, like the wind or running water.

"What if someone was trapped in that house? Trapped like Tommy, and I couldn't hear them or help them?" She wrapped her arms around her belly, bringing her knees up to her chest.

"You can't assume that. Besides, the family isn't scared, and there didn't seem to be anything really mean there." They'd actually been intrigued by the evidence Jessica found, certain their haunting was their grandfather who'd died of a heart attack in the house. He'd read stories to the children, now teenagers. It made them happy to think he might still be around, watching over them.

"Just because it's not malevolent doesn't mean it isn't scared and trapped," Jessica snapped back, getting angry.

He held up his hands. "Maybe we're looking at this the wrong way."

"What do you mean?" Her eyes narrowed, but she wasn't ready to launch nuclear airstrikes. She always took time to listen, even when furious.

"Maybe Tommy was like a case of beginner's luck. You stumbled on a situation where everything was tense and strong, and it sparked your gifts. The cases we've had since then haven't been anywhere near life-and-death. Now that you know it's possible, you can build up your strength and practice until you can see and hear ghosts in more ordinary circumstances." A few months ago, he would have cringed to hear those words coming out of his mouth, but now nothing mattered except restoring Jessica's confidence. Even if it meant keeping his own fears under wraps.

Jessica admitted she'd never dealt with anything like the demon box before. She hadn't even been able to see ghosts or entities before that night, despite coming from a long line of mediums. How could she be certain they'd actually contained the creature or even be sure it had all been driven out of Greg? That question had kept his eyes open and staring at the ceiling night after night.

He's still not telling me everything. Jessica wished she could talk to someone about Greg's continuing nightmares and increasingly short temper. They could be connected to the possession, but they could also be signs of recovery or ongoing problems. A traditional psychologist would never believe them, and the mediums she'd known through her mother weren't talking to her anymore. They either treated her like a competitor—not accepting that she hadn't inherited her mother's gifts—or they saw her work as a threat.

"Mom, if you're out there, I could really use your help." The words echoed around the empty apartment without a reply, not even a hint of a shiver across her skin. *I wonder if Mom ever tried to get in touch with me?* They'd argued about it right until her mother finally succumbed to the cancer that consumed her lungs. "You're my daughter, Jessie." Her mother had accused her of being too stubborn, too conservative, too wrapped up in wanting to be normal, never realizing that Jessica would have sold her soul for the chance to be special.

Had her mother tried and failed to reach her from the other side? Had she stood screaming in front of Jessica, invisible and silent to her daughter's stunted senses? The image sent icy chills skating across Jessica's skin. Had her mother given up? Or did she still believe that Jessica was deliberately ignoring her? Surely her mother would have been able to get through if she'd really wanted to. Even people without the gifts could sometimes see and sense ghosts.

"Enough depressing thoughts." She shook off her gloom and reached for her computer. Sheila, her manager at Billy's Breakfast Bar, had taken one look at the black eye and sent her home with a fistful of pamphlets for abuse hotlines. While Jessica appreciated the concern, she couldn't help feeling a little indignant that the woman hadn't believed her. Greg was not abusive. The guilt was tearing him up and twisting him in knots. *I have to find something to help him.*

"What I really need is an experienced medium, someone who has been dealing with spirits for a long time. Someone genuinely gifted." Jessica racked her memory, trying to come up with some possible names while the laptop booted up.

The screen blinked to life, presenting her with over forty different emails waiting for her attention. She began absently clicking through, deleting the promotional offers and invitations to collect money on behalf of Nigerian princes or to start her own mail-order business from home or find true love for a token fee. One email nearly went into the trash until she took a closer look.

From: cmann@afterlifeadventures.org To: info@gotghosts.com

Jessica,
You might not remember me, but your

mother and I used to be good friends
before she began her television show.

These days I manage a small bed and
breakfast, Rose on the Grave, in
partnership with Afterlife Adventures.

I'm sure you've heard of the recent
scandals involving faked phenomena at
some Afterlife locations. I'd like to hire
you to do an impartial investigations of
my facility, to show that we are not all
charlatans. I've been watching your career
for some time, and I know that you will be
honest.

If it is not inconvenient, please come to
Rose on the Grave this weekend as my
guest. I'm looking forward to reconnecting
with you.

Christie Mann

Mom? Is this your doing? She'd wished for
a reliable medium and now one had reached
out to her. Leaning back in her chair, Jessica
considered the offer. She'd heard of Afterlife
Adventures, along with everyone else in the
paranormal-investigations world. The owner,
Dennis Olegario, bought "haunted" properties
and converted them into tourist attractions,

charging high prices for otherworldly encounters. Last month, the quality of his franchise had been called into question when amateur investigators found electromagnets and hidden pneumatic tubes in two of the Afterlife sites. The owners had been using them to make objects appear to move by themselves.

Olegario loudly protested his innocence and expressed displeasure over the fraud perpetrated in his name. Usually this sort of thing wouldn't make any waves outside of the small world of those dedicated to the paranormal, but the government had taken notice. With more and more people getting excited about the bear-woman video on YouTube, they couldn't dismiss Afterlife Adventures as entertainment for kooks and weirdos, something to separate the gullible from their money.

An impartial investigation revealing undebunkable phenomena would certainly help. Jessica couldn't remember her mother ever mentioning a Christie Mann, though. A quick Internet search pulled up the photo of a middle-aged blonde in a pale purple peasant blouse. The face wasn't familiar, no matter how much Jessica pummeled her memory.

In the first few years of investigating, she'd drawn the attention of some of her mother's former colleagues. They'd accused her of siding with the skeptics who'd silenced her mother. But this invitation didn't feel like a trap. *Do I want to get caught up in the paranormal entertainment industry again?* This investigation could turn into something high profile, bringing all sorts of people out of the woodwork again.

Her mother's producers had pushed her to keep bringing up bigger and splashier results for her psychic readings. They'd never cared that the gift simply wasn't predictably reliable and rather than stand up for herself, her mother began supplementing her genuine talents with cold readings and guesswork. Jessica didn't want to make the same mistake. All she wanted was to be able to do her investigations properly and accurately, separating the natural from the supernatural. She could vindicate her mother, proving that the demands of the industry drove her to lie, not a desire to cheat her audience. Jessica wanted to know what was real and what was fraud, proving the truth of what her family had always insisted on: ghosts were real and very much among the living.

She began to type out an acceptance. If this Christie Mann was authentic, then maybe she'd be able to help Jessica achieve all her goals.

"You want to what now?" Greg stepped out of the shower, scowling and scrubbing a towel across his chest to dry himself. Jessica ignored his gruffness, enjoying the distracting sight of the man she loved wearing nothing but droplets of water. She'd half expected the intense attraction to fade as they got to know each other, but she still found herself with butterflies in her stomach every time she looked at him. She let her eyes roam over the broad expanse of his chest, lightly dusted with fine brown hair accenting the planes of muscles built from years of heavy hauling. It was like a map inviting a girl to touch and lick, guiding her across a delicious expanse of masculine beauty.

"Earth to Jess." The irritation faded from his voice. He liked watching her enjoy the view.

"What?" She protested innocently. *Stand firm now, climb him like a tree later.*

His lips twisted into a masculine smirk. "See something you like?"

She smiled back coyly, leaning back on the bed in a way that she knew thrust her breasts forward to their best advantage. "Maybe."

Any signs of the irritation were gone, leaving her with the Greg she knew and adored. He hung up the towel on its hook, standing in front of her in all his glory. "So where is it you want to go again?"

"Rose on the Grave, it's a haunted bed and breakfast. The owner knew my mother and has invited us up for a free weekend to investigate." Licking her lips, her mind rapidly sorted through incipient fantasies. And made note of Greg's definite interest.

"Sounds like trouble if you don't tell her what she wants to hear." He arched an eyebrow, attempting to look serious but not quite able to hide the lingering smirk.

He enjoyed knowing she found him attractive, and she suspected he was an exhibitionist. The way he prowled across the bedroom, glancing back to make sure she had a good view when he bent down to pick up his jeans, only added more proof to the theory. *A girl could bounce quarters off those cheeks.*

"I don't think so," said Jessica. "She said she chose me because she knew I'd be honest. Any of a dozen other investigators would be only too happy to validate whatever she wanted. They'd say the ghosts of Elvis and Marilyn Monroe were on permanent residency."

Irritation provided a potent antidote to her attraction. People who called themselves "investigators"—then insisted every grain of dust was a supernatural orb and called lens flares "manifestations"—didn't deserve to be considered in the same breath with her own careful scientific work.

"I'm up for any plans involving you and a bed." Greg recaptured her attention, pulling her against him so she could get the benefit of both sides of his double entendre. The jeans lay discarded across the bed.

I should make sure he was actually listening to

me… later. He hummed, nibbling at her throat with soft lips, the vibrations sending

powerful jolts of arousal straight through her body. Jessica gasped, digging her fingers into the bristly stubble covering his head when he hit the perfect sweet spot at the base of her neck.

"Like that?" He chuckled, and his smugness should have annoyed her. She promised herself she would remember to be annoyed, just as soon as he finished what he was doing.

He pushed up the hem of her loose skirt, tugging down her panties with one thick finger. Jessica bit back a moan, knowing she would have a hard time not remembering this moment every time she wore this outfit.

She didn't need much encouragement, anticipation had her swollen, wet, and ready. But she'd learned Greg did not like to skip over any preliminaries.

"Come on, baby. Show me what you like," he whispered in her ear, softly pressing her down against the bed. She clutched his broad, muscled back, trying to pull him tighter against her. He easily resisted her, supporting himself with one hand. He bent his head to slowly undo each button of her blouse with his teeth and lips.

After each parted button, he nuzzled her newly revealed skin, tracing a deliciously tortuous path down her enflamed body. He began to stroke between her parted thighs, finding her sensitive nub. She arched her back, desperate for completion.

"Shhh. Gotta prime the pump first." His grin widened his cheek against hers, but she couldn't share in his delight. She was so close. He teased her flesh, the rough calluses on his fingertips flicking across her in delightful friction. It didn't take much for her first orgasm to explode, making her writhe and moan.

"That's my girl. Now hold on tight." He eased himself into her, letting her pulsing folds draw him deeper and deeper inside.

Yesss. That was what she'd been waiting for. The satisfying fullness stretching her and giving her muscles something to clench. He rocked back and forth, each movement setting off a new wave of fireworks to ravage her body. She lost track of everything around her, sight, sound and sensation dissolving into a mirage of ecstasy.

Exhilarated satiation slowly drew her back into her body. Greg held her close, murmuring something softly, over and over. Her brain managed to put together enough power to make sense of it despite an overwhelming urge to simply collapse into a pleasure-coma.

"I love you, Jess. I'll never let myself hurt you." He kept repeating it, like a promise he didn't realize he was saying aloud.

Chill awareness cut through her afterglow. The nightmares he kept having, the ones which left him shaking and withdrawn. Were they about him hurting her? The tightness of his grip felt more desperate than reassuring when felt through her new mental filter.

"I know you'd never hurt me." She ran her fingers over his sweat-slicked prickly scalp.

His litany abruptly stopped. He pulled back, searching her expression for something.

Reassurance? Suspicion? She couldn't guess.

He got up and Jessica could almost see the brick and mortar growing higher behind his eyes. He smiled, but it was a pale imitation of his usual grin. He disappeared into the bathroom to clean up, leaving her to her own uncomfortable thoughts.

"This is it?" Greg scowled when they got out of the truck. His temper had become more brittle with each mile closer to the bed and breakfast.

Jessica couldn't blame him for being off-balance. Rose on the Grave was perfectly beautiful and charming, like an idealized image sitting in the dictionary beside the word *picturesque*. Yet with their feet planted on the pristine drive, that perfection became a weapon of intimidation, making her feel too flawed and grubby to be allowed to enter. The building used to be a church, and the original stone walls seemed to have soaked up a full share of solemn reverence, smothering laughter and smiles.

Heavy trees stood sentry, stretching out their limbs like prison bars across the overcast sky. Even the first buds dotting the black branches couldn't alleviate the chill of the rapidly cooling early-spring evening. A small graveyard stretched out beside the church, worn stones dotting a landscape of low bushes and carved stone benches. A garden of death, inspiring the Rose's name.

Goosebumps crept up her arms and back, a chill that had nothing to do with the late February air or the lengthening shadows from the sun's evening escape. Something wasn't right here. The sensation was distinctly less than the one from Greg's parents' home during its haunting by a demonic spirit, but powerful all the same. There were ghosts here; she felt certain of it. Maybe this would be the opportunity she'd hoped for, reigniting any mediumistic gifts inside her.

"They probably aren't even going to let us in looking like this." Greg's voice took on a sharp edge, slicing into Jessica's confidence. Now that they were here, the Rose looked more like a champagne-and-caviar type of place. Her worn jeans and black shirt were her typical investigation clothes since no one really cared what she wore in the dark. Greg's long-sleeved plaid flannel shirt and jeans were along the same lines.

Not welcome, the vines seemed to hiss with their rustling leaves. *Not one of us,* the trees whispered in the breeze. The cold stone monuments in the graveyard stabbed upward at the grey skies, stark reminders of the inevitability of death.

"We were invited." Jessica grabbed her courage and her equipment in both hands and walked up the winding flagstone path to the ornately carved wooden front door. The panels looked heavy and thick enough to withstand a medieval siege, but it swung open easily enough. The tiny front lobby inside was ornately patterned from the light of the jewel-toned abstract stained-glass windows set high in the wall.

A discreet bell announced their arrival, and a woman immediately bustled out of the office. Petite with wide blue eyes and a perky bob of ash-blonde hair, she appeared to be delighted to see them. She immediately seized Jessica's free hand, squeezing it eagerly.

"You look just like your mother did when she was a girl. It's uncanny." Christie's grin beamed brighter than the remnants of the late-day sunshine.

"Thanks." Jessica tried to offer a genuine smile in return, but the itching sensation crawling along her spine made it hard to relax.

The other woman's grip on Jessica's hand tightened. "She would be so proud of the work you've been doing. It takes real integrity to go against common thought and prove yourself right." Christie paused as if being reminded of her manners. "Oh my, I haven't introduced myself, have I? I'm Christie Mann. I'm sure you don't remember me. The last time I saw you was your fifth birthday party. I was one of the dozens of retro-hippie women wandering around in broomstick skirts."

Thankfully, Greg kept quiet while Jessica introduced them. She hoped Christie would assume his tight mouth and hard eyes were from the long trip, and tried to offset his sullenness with deliberate brightness. "I'm happy we were able to come out to help. We have our equipment in the truck."

"Wonderful. I'll take you around and show you the best places to set up." Christie linked her arm through Jessica's and began walking down the long nave. The pews had been removed and intimate tables for two and three were scattered throughout, the light from the stained glass painting their white tablecloths in soft colors. Their hostess steered them through a small door hidden between columns on the left wall.

"This is the most important room at the Rose. It used to be where they held Sunday school during church services." Christie ran her free hand along a worn wooden desk, greyed with age. Jessica looked around, trying not to wince. The weathered boards framing the walls and the threadbare carpets ground down by hundreds of visiting feet did nothing to dispel a chill hanging in the air. She wasn't an expert, but the re-created schoolroom looked authentic, with rows of desks against the wall and a selection of antique toys in the middle of the floor. The rocking horse with its plucked mane and faded paint, the unfinished wooden blocks making a fort for shiny tin soldiers, a few dark red hard rubber balls—they all could have come directly out of an illustration. It felt more like a shrine than a place where children once played.

"What happened?" Jessica asked, trying to get a sense of the room. Despite the oppressive atmosphere, this spot felt emptier than the rest of the church.

"It was a great tragedy. During services, candles set the wall between the church and this room on fire. The door is the only way out and the children were caught inside. The people in the church tried to break through the flames, but they couldn't. One father even tried to hack through the wall with an axe, but it was too late. All of the children died from the smoke." Christie's eyes teared up as if she'd personally lost someone in the century-old disaster. Jessica patted the hostess's arm in sympathy, ignoring

Greg's rolling eyes.

"When was this?" Greg asked, arms folded across his chest.

"1877, after Christmas," Christie replied promptly. "Many of the residents moved away after the tragedy, and the town stayed abandoned for almost fifty years. This church quickly acquired a reputation of being haunted, and no one wanted to hold services here. I bought it ten years ago with the help of Afterlife Adventures, then spent two years restoring it to its former glory." She patted the stone wall affectionately.

"Why didn't they go out the windows?" Greg pointed at the evenly-spaced openings filled with multiple narrow panes of glass.

"I beg your pardon?" Christie frowned. "The kids could have gotten out of the windows. And the wall between the church and this room is stone. It couldn't have caught fire."

Greg's observations were accurate but hardly sensitive. Jessica shot him a warning look.

To her surprise, Christie smiled. "I understand the confusion. The original structure didn't have windows. It was completely destroyed in the fire. I rebuilt it based on some sketches and plans on file at the courthouse. This room was originally a sort of lean-to and the community didn't have money for glass windows. It was lit with candles. I put in the windows so that the children wouldn't have to stay in the dark."

Christie didn't mention the stone wall, but Jessica supposed the fire could have started with some kind of fabric wall-hanging or nearby wooden furniture. She wouldn't press for details right now, and her glare warned Greg into doing the same. The sense of hostility crackling in the air intensified, once again leaving Jessica feeling like a target was aimed at her back.

"Most of the physical activity is in here," Christie continued. "I'd recommend a night-vision camera in this room." She tapped the top of the desk nearest the door.

"Are there any other hotspots?" Jessica hoped the change in topic would bring them back to more comfortable ground. The tension simmered so thickly that she couldn't imagine the others didn't feel it, particularly Christie, with her claims of sensitivity.

"We have a number of apparition sightings in the graveyard every year, and I get EVPs in the dining hall almost every night." Christie gestured back to the table-filled nave. "Four different EVPs have mentioned Gwen in the last two weeks."

Professional interest piqued, Jessica straightened. Gwen was one of the peculiarities of local ghost hunting back home. The name kept appearing in EVPs and other communications. No one had any idea what it meant or who this "Gwen" might be, but it was downright spooky to hear the name repeated in widely distant locations. Very few paranormal investigators published their results if Gwen was mentioned; it was sort of like keeping back crucial evidence to distinguish between the genuine cases and the hoaxes.

"Something has agitated our spectral residents. I know you must sense it. I'm not sure if they're offended by the accusations that they might not be real, or if they're reacting to something else. I've never had your mother's gift to communicate directly with them." Sadness pulled down the corners of Christie's lips.

"Me neither." Jessica sighed.

Christie's head snapped up. "I'm surprised to hear that."

"Mom was always disappointed I didn't inherit her gifts." Jessica suppressed an automatic instinct to curl into herself from embarrassment. She didn't need to be a medium to be a competent investigator.

"Oh, not that. But one of the reasons I called you was this." Christie pulled a small recorder out of her pocket and turned it on. Static hissed in the silence, popping and crackling. Jessica leaned closer.

"Tell Jessica to come. We need her help." A high-pitched voice, either a woman or a child, although the words were nearly lost in the background distortions.

Jessica swallowed. She'd asked her mother

for help. Had her ghost told her old friend to get in touch?

"I recorded it a few days ago. I'd been thinking of asking you for a while, even dreaming about it. But when I heard this, I knew time was of the essence." Christie fingered the slim metal box. "The ghosts have been misbehaving with the tourists, pinching and sending cold blasts at them. I actually cancelled the reservations for this weekend, hoping to give them a break."

"A break?" Greg asked, his voice sharp.

After what he'd been through, Jessica could imagine how unsettlingly it would be to be personally invited by the dead.

"Ghosts are just people. They want the same things we all want, to communicate and be acknowledged. Usually they crave the interaction with the guests. It makes them feel less alone." Christie looked around the empty room. "I know you've felt the hostility but trust me, it's much less than any other guests have been subjected to over the last few weeks. The children want you to be here."

Jessica unpacked their gear, laying it out on the small dresser. With only three night-vision cameras, she'd have to pick locations carefully. Or maybe we should carry them. She became aware of her shoulders creeping up to her ears and forced them back down with a frustrated sigh. She hadn't felt this vulnerable and targeted since she was the freak girl in high school, walking through halls lined with bullies and their mockery. If this was what it meant to be welcomed here, she didn't want to see what it felt like when that welcome wore out.

"Do you buy any of what she said?" Greg demanded, picking up the FLIR camera to check the battery.

"I don't know," Jessica admitted, settling on the vaguely Victorian king-sized bed. The room seemed like a typical bed-and-breakfast with its strange combination of anonymity trying to disguise itself in false hominess. Everything was a shade too put together to actually be personal. The few tables were cluttered with knickknacks and brochures for local tourist attractions. Only the room-darkening blinds were unusual, presumably installed in case guests wanted an in-room séance atmosphere. Or maybe just to help them sleep after a night of ghost-watching.

"I feel like I should have brought my tinfoil hat." Greg clicked the final battery pack into place. "That woman is flakier than a box of cereal."

"She's not wrong. There's something here. I can definitely feel it, and it's not happy." Jessica rubbed her arms, the goosebumps distorting her skin.

Greg paled. "Something like the demon box?"

Jessica shook her head. "This doesn't feel anything like the box. That entity was evil, oppressive, and coating everything. It liked making people miserable. This is more like"— she closed her eyes, trying to find the right words to share what she was feeling—

"Desperation and frustration."

"You sure?" His voice cracked, hoarse and rough.

"I'm sure." She wrapped her arms around him. His body was rock hard with tension, and not the good kind. She couldn't blame him for his doubts, but she was certain. She'd never sensed anything like the entity in the demon box in all her years of paranormal investigations. Whatever lingered here wasn't another inhuman entity. She didn't know what it was, but it seemed to be much more in line with the subtle tension and presence she'd felt at other hauntings.

Greg exhaled, and she felt a slight softness loosen his rigid muscles. "So, what's the plan?"

"Look around, see what we can see tonight. Then talk to Christie in the morning, if you can restrain yourself." She stole a quick kiss on his chin, hoping to sweeten his surly mood.

"You can't expect me to take her seriously." His large hands wrapped around her waist, pulling her close.

"She's not any different from me," Jessica warned. Greg raised one eyebrow.

"I see a few differences."

"She cares about what she's doing." Jessica pulled back, folding her arms over her chest.

"She's running a business that depends on her finding what she and her clients want to see. Her livelihood depends on it. You've never put yourself in a position where you have to choose between a paycheck and the truth," Greg pointed out, his blue eyes harsh with judgment.

"That doesn't make her a fraud," Jessica replied. "It makes her suspect. And it's why she needs you."

Greg offered a sly smile. "She must think she really has something or else she'd be calling one of the others."

Jessica tried to maintain a sober expression. "Flattering me isn't going to get you out of trouble."

"Not even a little?" He grinned. "Come on, cut me some slack. This is still new for me."

"Which is why you're going to behave and keep your eyes and ears open, but your mouth shut." She allowed him to tug her back into his arms, resting her cheek against his broad shoulder. For a moment, she could pretend that everything was the way it had been when they first met, when they were just a man and a woman. Before the box and everything that had come crawling out of it.

"Just call me Mr. Big Brother," he teased, holding her tightly.

Reluctantly, Jessica pulled away. She wanted the moment to last, but she had a job to do, and the night was ticking away. Greg took two of the night-vision cameras while she pocketed the recorder for EVPs and grabbed the last night-vision camera and the FLIR.

The sense of unearthly presences was even stronger when they stepped into the long hall housing the guest suites. Moonlight cut harsh outlines against the wall and floor, slashing the shadows but making them even darker, as if the light were forcing the darkness to condense. Despite the sense of lurking disapproval, Jessica sensed an impression of staleness and lingering history. Whatever she was getting wasn't something here now but something that had left its mark and had long since departed. The footprint rather than the boot.

Christie met them at the door where the guest quarters joined the church, her dark clothes blending with the shadows while her blond hair caught the silvery light. It made her look like an apparition, a floating head, and Jessica cynically wondered if it was a deliberate effect.

The three of them went to the schoolroom, none breaking the imposed silence. With pointed fingers, Jessica showed Greg where to set up his two cameras so they could have multiple angles of the room. Giving him the FLIR, she directed him to sit with his back against the stone wall of the church.

Nodding, Greg turned on the camera and did a preemptive pan of the room, documenting what was already present. Jessica turned on her camera, ready to begin.

The room and its contents appeared on the tiny screen in green-limned necrotic detail. "This is a Spirit Sight investigation into phenomena at Rose on the Grave. There are three people present: myself, Greg, and Christie, the owner of the Rose. No one else is in the building at this time. Traffic on the road outside is minimal, but the rural location means we must consider wildlife when searching for possible potential explanations for any phenomena. The time is currently 8:47 p.m. and we will start with an EVP session, with the owner's permission."

Jessica turned the camera on Christie. The other woman's face was eerily pale, and her eyes were black hollows. Her bony hand gestured for them to proceed. Jessica took the recorder out of her pocket and put it on the floor in the center of the room, cushioning it with a book so it wouldn't pick up the vibrations from their movements as they shifted weight.

Bracing her elbow against her ribs to keep the camera steady, Jessica began the session. "Is there anyone present here who would like to speak with us?"

Silence stretched out. Jessica silently counted to twenty in her head. First rule of EVPs—make sure to leave plenty of room for a delayed response. But somehow, she doubted there would be anything on the recording except static. There was no sense of an aware and responsive entity.

"Can you give us a sign of your presence?" Something to help her to feel that she wasn't talking to an empty room.

A soft rustle caught their attention. Jessica slowly panned the camera until she found the open book lying on the desks lining the opposite wall. One of the pages slowly lifted, quietly scraping against the others still lying in place. The moving page rolled and then flicked into place on the opposite side, exactly like an invisible hand turning the page.

Jessica hardly dared to breathe in case the movement fouled the recording. A second page lifted and turned, then it quickly flipped back to its previous position. Which meant this couldn't possibly be the result of an unfelt breeze or draft ruffling the pages. Air didn't abruptly switch directions, not without the people in the room feeling the change.

And yet her blunted senses weren't picking up anything. Disappointment swelled, shoving hard against her ribcage and mind, filling her with its hollow ache. Here she stood, witnessing one of the clearest phenomena she'd ever seen outside of Greg's parents' haunting, and she couldn't even summon up the rudimentary level of sensitivity she'd managed for most of her life.

Stay professional. Taking a deep breath, Jessica continued with the EVP. "Christie says you're sad. That you don't want to talk to people anymore. Is that true?"

Wood grated on wood in reply. Jessica lowered the camera to the antique rocking horse, now slowly shifting back and forth.

Conflicting excitement and uncertainty churned, so she looked at Greg, wondering what he was thinking. He knelt on the floor, one hand holding the FLIR steady on the horse while the other spread his fingers widely on the worn wooden planks.

"It's not the floor warping or movement under the substructure," he said quietly.

"Of course not, it's my children." Christie beamed, holding out her hands as if offering a maternal blessing. "Tell us what we can do for you, darlings. What do you need?"

The horse continued to rock, and a small rubber ball rolled along the floor, bouncing slightly, the same way it would if it had been kicked by an unseen foot. Jessica clamped her free hand over her camera hand, trying to keep the recording steady. She took another deep breath and reminded herself that she could deal

116

with her feelings later. For now, she needed to document everything. She lifted her eyes from the tiny screen, hoping to re-center herself, and met the eyes of a little boy staring in at her from outside the window, his pale face indistinguishable from the glare of moonlight.

"Who's that?" Jessica swung the camera to the window. But the green-lit screen showed only empty glass.

"Who?" Christie asked, a hint of irritation pinching her voice. The toys abruptly ceased moving.

"There was a boy at the window." Or had her mind played tricks on her? Making a face out of random shadows and light.

Greg quickly went to the window and peered outside, scanning with the FLIR and his own eyes. "I'm not seeing any evidence of a heat signature."

Jessica stood perfectly still, the first prickling of embarrassment beginning to sink kitten claws into her cheeks. If someone had been there, even if that person ran away too quickly for them to see, there would have been lingering heat impressions from where they'd stood. No heat signature, no intruder.

"It must have been one of the children." Christie's jubilation abruptly folded into a frown. "But why would he be outside? Oh dear, we'll have to find out. I'm sure the children are tired from their efforts and would like to rest now."

It was a polite dismissal but held more than a taste of triumphant vindication. Jessica couldn't blame her. The phenomena at the Rose were more intense than any other haunting that she had ever seen, except the box incident. Normally, she would be excited, eager to check out the graveyard or the dining hall for further phenomena. Instead, she felt drained and like an imposter. *I really thought my gifts were starting to wake up.*

A stubborn part of her mind insisted she didn't need psychic gifts. She'd spent years documenting paranormal phenomena with nothing more than the typical human senses. But this struck hard at her childhood memories of watching her mother speak to apparently empty air, of feeling left out and unimportant. *Of feeling like I was somehow defective or broken because I couldn't do what she did.*

Greg came to her rescue, providing a professional escape. "Hey, it's been a long drive and a long day. Why don't we call it an early evening? We can do more tomorrow after we review the footage."

Unwilling to trust her voice, Jessica silently knelt to pick up the recorder and turn it off. Based on what she'd seen, no doubt it was full of clear and relevant communications. All without her ever sensing a single ghost.

Greg slowly crept out of bed, his anger and frustration driving spurs into him and making it impossible to stay asleep any longer. He wanted to run down the hall to Christie's bedroom and drive his fist into her sanctimonious, pretentious face for putting Jessica through this kind of humiliation. The strength of his reaction disconcerted him. He'd never been particularly Neanderthalish before. His heart might be breaking at the sight of Jessica trying to be brave while hiding how hurt she was at how the investigation had turned out, but he'd never been one to resort to violence. Slamming a hammer into a bent nail didn't fix anything and neither would slamming fists.

I wish we hadn't come here. Maybe he should have tried to convince Jessica to give up Spirit Sight when she'd first become frustrated at not being able to sense ghosts the way she had at his parents' house. He had spoken to some of her investigator friends, and they'd noticed

differences, too. She used to take a lot of pride in her work. Now each investigation spritzed lemon juice into an open wound.

He tweaked aside the blinds to stare at the rosy clouds hovering on the eastern horizon. New day, new beginnings, but he couldn't stop the dread from poisoning his thoughts. He needed a distraction.

Pulling out his laptop, Greg decided to do a little research. Something about Christie's story of a tragic fire didn't quite ring true. Maybe he'd get lucky and the local archives would be available online.

Google happily spit back a plethora of references to his initial query. Clicking on the links, it seemed as if every local paper and television station inside a hundred-mile radius happily repeated the story for Hallowe'en filler. Rose on the Grave was listed in several *Top Ten Spooky Stays* lists and had a large number of raving reviews.

Then there were the stories about Afterlife Adventures and the scandal of faked phenomena. The local residences were quick to defend their tourist lure with lots of "we don't do that kind of thing here" rhetoric. Christie featured in a number of interviews, sharing her tragic tale, reiterating that her goal was to provide a home for those unsettled spirits and whatever stimulation was still possible. She didn't want her little horde of undead children to be bored and restless, ready to cause trouble. Instead, she hoped to give them a place of security and acknowledgment, so they would eventually be able to move on.

Christie had uttered all the right noises, yet something still rang false to Greg. He ran his hand over his scalp, all too aware he wasn't exactly a neutral observer anymore. He couldn't rely on his gut; he needed real evidence one way or another. He found the local library, which promised to have archived copies of old newspapers on microfiche.

Should I tell her? He paused to look at Jessica, curled up under the heavy quilt, her mouth and eyes tight, even in her sleep. She didn't need this additional burden. If he was right, he'd find a discreet way to share it with her. If not, then he'd have to accept that he really was just paranoid. The decision dragged heavily on him, pulling him further away from the woman he loved. He needed the space to repair his calm if he ever wanted to get back to being the kind of man she deserved.

His hands itched for his tools. He wanted to carve, stain, or assemble—anything to keep his fingers busy and free his mind and heart. But he doubted Christie would appreciate his efforts, if he began an unauthorized early-morning renovation on her property.

Instead, he awkwardly tilted the large TV and turned it on at the lowest volume. Maybe he could find something to distract him. He picked a random channel and saw a flash of the President speaking. Before Greg could figure out what the man was talking about, the clip shifted to several women sitting around a table.

A tall blonde spoke immediately. "This

sounds more like a joke than a Presidential announcement, but April Fool's is still over a month away."

The statuesque brunette next to her shook her head. "I don't think we can dismiss this so easily. People have been sharing all kinds of stories—"

"People always share stories about UFOs and Bigfoot, too," interrupted a stylish woman with a colorful headwrap. "They aren't any more real than these people with so-called strange and unusual abilities."

"How can you deny the evidence?" the brunette shot back. Greg switched the channel and found a morning newscast.

"The President's announcement yesterday has generated a great deal of uncertainty." The sober news anchor stared earnestly into the camera as if warning every viewer. "Some are celebrating the government finally acknowledging a potential threat while others are deriding the President as gullible and a fearmonger. No one seems convinced of the need for this new government agency, the Bureau of Special Investigations. People are asking where the money will come from to fund it, what will they do to protect ordinary citizens, and most importantly, what will their mandate be. The White House is surprisingly short on answers to these questions."

Greg turned off the television, his heart

thumping in his ears. Fumbling with his laptop, it took an agonizingly long time to connect with the Rose's Wi-Fi. His mind kept racing. The President couldn't be talking about people like Jessica, could he?

Finally, he found an online video of the President's announcement. "Thank you for coming. I'll be brief and will not be accepting any questions. Of late, we have all grown concerned with the recent claims of strange and unusual activity. We created a special investigative task force to investigate these claims and to our surprise, some of them have turned out to have some substance. In response to this information, I am creating a new enforcement agency to deal with such individuals, the Bureau of Special Investigations. Further information about this agency will be provided at the end of this conference. I want to reassure the American people that we are not taking this new threat lightly, and that they do not need to worry. Thank—"

What the hell is that supposed to mean? Greg clicked off the screen. Deal with? Was Jessica in danger? His Neanderthalish instincts suggested now would be a great time to invest in some subterranean cave-esque real estate.

"Hey, bad dreams?" Jessica's sleepy voice interrupted the growing stream of panic.

Greg turned the computer around. "I think you need to see this."

"No EVPs? Well, the children aren't always feeling talkative." Christie patted a headstone affectionately while she and Jessica walked through the garden graveyard.

Jessica was less sanguine about the hours of empty recordings. Granted, she'd been somewhat distracted, thinking about the President's announcement. It still seemed too surreal to really understand the implications. She and Greg had spent six hours going through the different recordings from last night, visual and audio, and she'd never seen results like these.

The visual evidence was stunning. They'd captured movement of the book, horse, and ball from multiple angles. The ball was particularly impressive, sitting quietly on the floor beside a basket of other toys before abruptly lurching into motion without any visible means of propulsion. Nothing fell on it or near it and none of them had been close enough to move it.

But not a single EVP or sign of an apparition. And no tingles of a ghostly presence aside from the brief flash of the boy at the window. That had never happened in all of Jessica's years of investigating. She swallowed around the lump in her throat, remembering the argument she and Greg had gotten into. He insisted there must be some kind of trick and wanted to confront Christie. She'd tried to get him to see the need to be diplomatic. Accusing their host of fraud based solely on Jessica's unreliable senses would ruin her reputation as an investigator. They needed to find out more.

"Is that typical here? To have a physical manifestation without an apparition or EVP?"

"It happens sometimes. I tend not to put much stock in it, though," said Christie, waving her hand dismissively before shoving it back into her pocket. Spring might be well underway, but the afternoon sun still held the bite of winter past.

"Why not?" Most people wanted something physical they could put on their websites or post to their followers.

"It's not really a true communication. And it's the easiest phenomena to fake. In my opinion, the most valuable experiences are when there is direct communication between the living and dead. Those are the encounters that will convince people that the dead need protection, just like the living."

Christie's enthusiasm reassured Jessica. Their opinions matched, and the other woman seemed to be much more interested in protecting her ghosts than exploiting them. But one word surprised her. "Protection? I don't understand. The dead deserve respect and we should certainly help spirits who are trapped, but what sort of protection would they need?"

"The group that initially bought this church planned to demolish it and put up a hotel. They had a number of accidents on the site." Christie touched the grey stone bench, checking to make sure it was dry before sitting down. "Machines would stop working when they arrived, people would drop tools. There were strange noises and apparitions, frightening the workers. It caught my attention, and I came down here. A local woman told me about the fire, and then it became clear to me that the ghosts didn't want to have their home disturbed."

Jessica nodded. She'd seen the phenomena before. Renovation seemed to stir up lingering spirits and often preceded hauntings at otherwise quiet sites.

"I didn't have the money to buy the place myself, but I got in touch with Mr. Olegario, and he immediately arranged to purchase it from the very frustrated owners. Then he funded the restoration. I oversaw every stage, and there were no further problems. If the rights of the dead were recognized, then no one would think of taking away their homes." Christie smiled at the stone walls warmed by the late morning sunshine.

"Do you really think people will see it that way?" It could make estate sales into a nightmare.

"People are finally starting to accept that the world is far more complicated than we've wanted it to be. Look how many people are accepting the video of that woman transforming. And the announcement yesterday is a step in the right direction. It will make it much easier to separate the frauds from authentic hauntings." Christie's warm smile took on a hint of vindictiveness, as if she'd be more than happen to prosecute.

Jessica was more cautious. "A lot of people are afraid. They don't know what to think."

"Shifting worldviews isn't easy, and people are always afraid. They mocked Jenner for trying to vaccinate people against smallpox. John Snow faced tremendous backlash for suggesting that cholera came from tainted water in the heart of London. They persevered against the opposition and lives everywhere were improved by better understanding what they were dealing with. It's why what you do is so valuable, Jessica. Your evidence helps to silence the doubters." Christie patted the bench beside her.

The stone was chilly but not achingly cold. Jessica decided to use Christie's compliment as a segue to more questions. "All I've ever wanted was to help uncover the truth, whatever it is. I know ghosts are real, but it's hard to convince other people with all the faked phenomena floating around out there. I feel like a racehorse loaded down with extra weights."

"How so?" Christie asked.

"If I had my mother's talents, I would be able to see when ghosts are present, letting me home in on reliable and incontrovertible evidence of hauntings." Jessica explained what she had seen at Greg's parents' home, the difficulties she'd experienced since, and her hopes that Christie would know the exercises her mother recommended for strengthening psychic gifts. She only left out Greg's possession by the Bad Thing.

The older woman was silent for a good while, long enough for Jessica to wonder if she'd inadvertently offended her. When Christie finally spoke, all traces of the generous hostess were gone. "What you've said is very troubling. Inhuman entities such as the one you describe from this demon box are dangerous."

"If I'd have known it was more than a normal haunting, I wouldn't have tried to deal with it. But once I was there, I couldn't walk away. Who knows what it could have done?" Jessica's spine stiffened at the implication of incompetence.

"Of course. And you did the best you could. The creature probably jammed open your psychic abilities, hoping to use your body. You're lucky it didn't get in. Once inside, an entity like that is almost impossible to entirely dislodge." Christie studied the tiny slivers of green beginning to poke through the dark ground.

"More than ever, I'm convinced your mother arranged for us to meet. She knew that I needed your help and that I could help you in turn."

Christie's words tightened the secret screws holding down the lid on Jessica's concerns about Greg, increasing the pressure.

"Let's start with going through some preliminary awareness exercises," Christie directed. "There are always lots of presences in the graveyard. Close your eyes and take deep steady breaths."

Obeying, Jessica relaxed into a comfortable position. With her eyes closed, she became more aware of her other senses. The rich scent of the thawing ground and renewed plant growth filled her nostrils. Faint chirps from the first intrepid birds laying claim to nesting territory.

"One by one, examine your physical senses and try to move beyond them." Christie guided her, the rhythmic rise and fall of her voice helping Jessica to relax even more. She could sense the other woman beside her in a way that was difficult to put into words. A sense of heaviness, of space being occupied, the sensation was a primal awareness that probably dated back to when detecting an intruder could be a life-saving trait.

Christie wasn't the only presence. Hers was the most dynamic, but Jessica could sense other, dimmer presences flickering on the edge of her abilities. Like trying to see stars in the same sky with the sun, it was more of an impression than a definite confirmation.

It still wasn't clear like Tommy's EVP. Jessica pushed her awareness outward and felt a definite reaction from one of the flickers. It began to drift closer, and she got a sense of great age and maleness. "I think I've found one. An old man?"

The flicker vanished at her words, and Jessica had the abrupt sensation of someone slamming a door in indignation. "He's gone."

"That's a good start." Christie's words of praise soothed. "What you might be feeling is an echo rather than an aware spirit."

Jessica was familiar with the phenomenon. She'd seen any number of hauntings that didn't react to people or attempt to communicate. Echoes of the past.

"Don't try to push it too hard. It takes a long time to develop psychic senses, just like any other kind of exercise." Christie patted Jessica's knee. "Practice every day. I've always preferred graveyards. The dead here are quieter, less frantic."

"Mom used to say that, too." She would have liked the Rose. The trees surrounding the graveyard would be beautiful once new leaves filled out their outstretched canopies. The garden plots between and around graves might be mostly bare ground now, but it would be lovely once plants bloomed along the flagstone paths and grave markers. Jessica could imagine it full of color and scent, with butterflies flitting between sunlight and shadow. "She said the ghosts in graveyards were content to enjoy the views until they faded."

"Exactly. I envied her for the clarity of her gifts, you know. At least until what happened with the show." Christie clicked her tongue in disappointment. "She deserved better than that."

"It's why I started investigating. It made me so angry when people dismissed everything she did as fraud." Jessica surprised herself at the depth of simmering anger in her voice. She thought she'd come to terms with it a long time ago.

She wasn't alone in her frustrations.

Christie's beatific expression twisted into a furious knot. "We are a profession that has always been rife with frauds. The old spiritualists thought they were 'helping' the spirits with their antics, but the tricks cast disrepute onto the whole profession. It didn't matter how many otherwise inexplicable phenomena there were, people could always point to the fakes."

Sir Arthur Conan Doyle. Her mother always referred to him as an example. He'd been so eager to believe, he'd publicly endorsed several frauds, which ended his career and authority. This made belief in ghosts more of a punchline than an opportunity for serious investigation.

"I suspect Mr. Olegario is now wishing he'd listened to me about trusting to the spirits rather than installing enhancements," Christie said with a sigh. "I'm not sure if Afterlife Adventures will be able to recover from these discoveries, even if people are more open to the unexplainable than ever before."

"What will happen to the Rose if Afterlife shuts down?"

Christie didn't seem worried. "It depends on how quickly it folds. Long drawn-out court cases or lawsuits could leave us vulnerable. I intend to use your evidence as part of a claim to sever the Rose from Afterlife Adventures, making us an independent facility."

They'd lose potential advertising and referrals from Afterlife, but with the company in chaos, there wouldn't be many of those anyway. Jessica couldn't blame her.

"I'd be glad to help however I can."

"Thank you. You and I have a lot in common"—Christie hesitated—"I hope you won't think I'm sticking my nose in, but I'm concerned about your young man. I know that no one likes to hear warnings when they're in love, but…"

Jessica made herself take a deep breath rather than angrily defending Greg when Christie trailed off. "But?"

"You say he wasn't a believer. Then he

became the subject of a rather intense paranormal experience, one which would have unsettled even a highly-experienced investigator. And if I'm not mistaken, this is his handiwork." Christie lightly touched the darkening bruise around Jessica's eye. Clearly the makeup didn't disguise it enough.

"It was an accident. He had a nightmare," Jessica said defensively, well aware that her words sounded like the excuses every abused woman had used in the history of time.

"I see." Christie's polite smile made Jessica want to start babbling to prove Greg's innocence, but she held her tongue. Their connection was strong, but she didn't really know him well enough or long enough to be certain his behavior was atypical. It left Jessica exhausted, being torn between her heart and the cynical parts of her brain. If the bad moods, flashes of anger, and nightmares were a result of his possession, she couldn't abandon him. But if this was who he truly was, she needed to leave and quickly. Every incident eroded her confidence in their relationship, yet the decision still seemed impossible.

"People can be affected by dark energy. Something like this demon box would have been very powerful." Christie clasped her hands over her crossed knees. "Perhaps Greg had more exposure than you realized at the time, and some spiritual cleansing is in order."

Hope surged. Here was a way to resolve the issue once and for all. "Could you help with that?"

"Of course, dear." Christie laughed as if it had never been in question. "If he'd been possessed it would be different, of course."

Hope was painful when it deflated. Jessica forced her stiff lips into a smile. *A cleansing will help. It has to.* "Right. Of course."

"All right, ghosts, let's see what you got," Greg muttered, kneeling beside the vintage rocking horse. Its faded and patchy rose paint still showed traces of hand-painted dapples on the back. Real wiry horse hairs spiked out of the gap running along the back of its neck, though the tail had long since vanished. A polished leather bridle and saddle gleamed, obviously new additions.

After his fight with Jessica, he'd spent long and frustrating hours going through screen after screen of the local weekly newspaper. He learned about litters of puppies that escaped and frolicked through the main square, then read excruciating details of weddings, funerals, garden parties—and who wore what to which. What he hadn't found was any mention of a fire destroying the church and killing children. Not in 1877 or any year in the decade surrounding it. Not at Christmastime or any other season. There was no record of it, and he had to believe that a paper who dedicated an entire front page to Mrs. Ogilvie's superior pumpkin soup recipe would have covered such a catastrophe.

The librarian told him the town's population was decimated in the 1918 flu pandemic, with almost a third of the occupants dying within a few months. The church had been abandoned shortly after, based on the announcement that residents would have to go to the next town for services. The reputation of it being haunted grew sometime in the forties, with each generation of schoolchildren trying to frighten the next with horrible tales.

Which meant that Christie Mann was lying through her smiling teeth. And she would drag Jessica down with her unless Greg could figure out how the woman was faking her effects.

He pushed gently on the wooden horse's chest, wanting to see how easily it moved. As expected for such a carefully crafted child's toy, the superb balance required very little effort to set it rocking. So, what could Christie use to start it? He'd seen a number of ghost-debunking videos where people used electromagnets or pneumatic tubes to cause objects to move. After spending nearly an hour scouring the walls for tiny openings to allow bursts of compressed air, he'd come to the conclusion that it must be a magnet.

He ran his fingers over the cool paint, trying not to dislodge any flakes. When he checked the back haunch, his fingers detected a thin, almost imperceptible gap. Leaning close, he used a magnifying glass and found a narrow, irregular seam. It had been done very carefully and camouflaged to look like a crack in the paint. But now that he'd spotted it, he wondered how anyone else had missed it. It was like getting a peek at how a magic trick was done. Once seen, it couldn't be unseen.

Of course, the seam could be anything. It could be repair work to replace a damaged section. The only way to find out would be to open it. Greg's fingers flexed around his not-a-screwdriver, the heavy flat-headed tool he used whenever he needed to pry something open or dig into something or any of the other hundred practical non-screw-turning tasks that were sometimes necessary. He hated the idea of damaging such a superb piece of craftsmanship, but he couldn't allow Christie to ruin Jessica's professional reputation. He also couldn't let Jessica beat herself up for not sensing spirits at what looked more and more like a fraudulent setup. The memory of her downturned face gave him courage, and he set the tip of the screwdriver blade to the seam.

The plug popped out easier than he'd expected, flipping open like a plastic battery cover. The wood clattered on the floor, scattering rose paint chips. A metal disk shone, nestled in a tiny cavity beneath the plug. The metal screwdriver pulled toward it proving it was magnetic.

"Gotcha." Greg's lips stretched in bitter triumph. "Now where's your partner?" The matching electromagnet would have to be nearby to be effective. Maybe under the desk?

"What are you doing?" Christie's shriek wasn't otherworldly, but it still caused him to jump, banging his head on the desk.

Pain clenched his eyes closed, driving red hot spikes through his skull.

"Greg, are you okay?" Jessica's voice came closer, and her cool hands began probing through his hair.

He winced away. He must have really clocked himself for it to hurt this badly. *Should have worn a hard hat.* He made himself open his eyes, blinking to clear away the film blurring his vision.

"You've destroyed it!" Christie's second shriek had him wondering if maybe he should have kept his eyes closed.

He growled. "I'm not the one who hid magnets inside it, lady."

"What?" Jessica frowned, looking at the horse as if she hadn't seen it before. She touched the little button magnet.

"That was an antique! I spent months

searching for it during the restoration." Christie still wasn't ready to focus on the big picture. "It was the one they wanted. The one they kept showing me."

"Then why is this hidden inside?" Irritation sharpened Jessica's voice. Good girl. Greg knew he could trust her to handle it while he tried to figure out if he'd given himself a concussion.

"You of all people should understand, Jessica," Christie sniffed. "Mr. Olegario doesn't like to risk tourist disappointment."

"So, he installed a magnetic pair to fake phenomena." Jessica folded her arms, her words falling with the finality of a gavel bang. Case closed.

Greg smiled proudly, ready to watch her rip into the smug hostess.

"Yes, and I disabled every single one of them immediately after his visit." Christie replied indignantly, her nose lifting into the air.

Greg sat up in surprise. "Wait. You did what?"

"I disabled them. I knew I didn't need that kind of assistance. There was a pairing magnet hidden there, under the desk. I threw it away, but I couldn't remove that one without damaging the horse. I couldn't do that to the children. They've already suffered so much." Christie glared at him. "You've completely ruined it."

"You should have mentioned this when you

first hired us. We could have helped you to find any remaining guarantees and eliminate them." Jessica didn't look quite ready to wave the flag on her righteous anger, but Greg could hear the doubt creeping in. Guilt crushed him more painfully than the desk's impact with his skull. He should have gone to her rather than rushing to investigate on his own.

"It was years ago. I found them all without your help." Christie sniffed. "I was certainly not going to allow myself to be labelled a fraud simply because a businessman is too impatient and greedy to understand that my ghosts are not dancing ponies to perform on demand."

"I'm, ah, sorry." Greg picked up the wooden plug, his confidence vanishing like solid ground in an earthquake. "I'll take the magnet out and glue the wood back."

Christie snatched the slim wooden piece out of his hands. "You've done enough. I've seen you rolling your eyes at me. Because only an 'idiot' would believe in ghosts."

Jessica straightened, anger tightening her face. "Hold on. That's not called for. You asked us to investigate. He might have overstepped, but he was doing his job. Lots of so-called mediums use these tricks, which is why we have to investigate in the first place."

"Investigate." Christie hissed.

"Wandering around with your little cameras, casting judgment on things you couldn't possibly understand. Neither of you will ever sense the wonders that I can. No wonder your mother resorted to fraud."

Jessica blinked, then her fingers slowly curled into fists. When she finally spoke, her voice was cold enough to flash-freeze. "I see. We'll be on our way, then."

Humiliated, Jessica watched the Rose on the Grave grow smaller in the side mirror. Scrunched down in the passenger seat, she kept running her fingers over the tight ridges of the seatbelt. The sun sank low to the horizon behind them, coloring everything in red and gold.

"On a scale of one to ten, how mad are you?" Greg asked.

Jessica sighed, resting her forehead against the cool glass. "Depends. Which end is which on the scale?"

"One is: 'Gee, I'm glad we had an excuse to leave.' Ten is: 'I'm planning to smother you in your sleep tonight.'" His knuckles tightened around the steering wheel.

"About a seven-point-three. And I wouldn't smother you in your sleep." Jessica allowed a small smile to briefly surface through the depression. It felt like it had been months since she could genuinely smile. "I've never been kicked off a site before." His reflection in the glass winced. "I'm really sorry, Jess. I should have come to talk to you first."

"Why didn't you?" She rolled her head around to look at him directly.

His fingers tightened on the wheel. "I found out that she'd lied about the fire. And I got it in my head to find out what else she lied about. It all seemed logical and reasonable at the time, and now I can't even remember why."

It didn't sound like the man she'd come to know. Was it a mistake in judgment or a sign of something more sinister? Jessica wished she could be certain which. She reached over and clicked on the radio.

"Guess we'll just have to have our own romantic weekend without the distraction of an investigation?" His big hand wrapped around her fingers, gently squeezing.

She tried to summon up the appropriate enthusiasm, but her emotions were tangled in too many tight knots for the idea of sex to seem appealing. She nodded and ended up yawning halfway through.

His thumb rubbed over her hand. "I'm sorry. You must be wiped. Try to get some sleep. It's a long drive back to the city."

Avoiding making a decision sounded good, and maybe a nap would help her gain more perspective. Her physical and emotional reserves were exhausted. She relaxed back into the truck seat, her eyes drifting shut.

"Jeez Louise, you deaf or something, lady?" an irritated child complained.

Jessica opened her eyes, unsurprised to see a young boy standing in front of her. I'm dreaming, she mused, scanning the empty horizon. Just herself and the boy in a vast three-dimensional field of soft grey.

"I been trying to talk to you since yesterday! Thought you was supposed to be a sensitive type." He scowled, yanking his flat cap lower on his head.

Jessica shrugged. "I guess I'm not cut out to follow in my mother's footsteps." This realization didn't hurt so much in a dream. If she wasn't a psychic, if seeing Tommy was some kind of one-time fluke, right now it didn't seem like such a bad thing. She could still do her job. It didn't change anything about her.

"Then how the heck are we finally talking?" The boy ran his thumbs along the inside of his dark grey suspenders.

"I'm not talking. I'm dreaming. Coming to terms with my disappointment." Jessica turned away from the strange boy to scan the horizon again. Her dreams weren't usually this bare. The ones she remembered were jam-packed full of odd details.

"Do I look like a dream to you?"

Actually, he didn't. At least, not one Jessica

was familiar with. He resembled an extra from a Depression-era movie, which wasn't a period of time she'd spent any thought on. Why would her subconscious create him instead of an image of her mother or Greg or Christie or someone else connected with her life? Why create a twelve-year-old strange boy?

"Who are you?"

"The name's Chuck. You need to turn this van around and go back to that church place." He pointed to his right.

Jessica peered, but there was nothing there. "Why? So I can finish what I started, and leave no stone unturned? So I can find my own path?"

He shouted back at her. "So you can save Bernie!"

I don't know anyone called Bernie. This dream was starting to be odd enough to warrant professional intervention.

"I tried to tell her about the trouble on its way. Lots of strange stuff going down and people trying to seem important. She told her mom, but her mom don't listen to us. She thinks it's all some kinda game." Chuck flickered, reappearing in front of her, his grey eyes wide and his mouth twisted tight. "If they'd'a listened to me, then Shawna wouldn't have gotten arrested. And now you think I'm some kinda freaking dream!"

"It's my dream. I can think whatever I

143

want," Jessica insisted, despite the sliver of doubt pricking at her awareness. There were too many inconsistencies, too many unique details. Like Chuck's shoes. She'd never seen shoes like that outside of a historical movie.

"You have to listen to me! Bernie needs help." Chuck's desperation finally broke through the muffling calmness wrapped around Jessica's mind, jolting her awake.

The sun had set, and Greg was pulling up to a traffic light. Jessica blinked in confusion, trying to sort the too-realistic dream memories into their appropriate mental slots.

"Hey, you okay? It's barely been an hour." Greg frowned, his fingers tightening on the wheel.

Jessica rubbed at her eyes. The dream had seemed so real. "We need to go back."

"You're sure he said Bernie?" Christie asked, her pink nails tapping against the desk. She hadn't been happy to see them returning and only relented when Jessica passed on Chuck's message.

Jessica took a deep breath. Begging this woman to give her a second chance had been humiliating, but she couldn't get Chuck's desperate plea out of her head.

"Yes. I know it sounds like a dream—"

"It sounds like a visitation," Christie interrupted. "I've heard the name Bernie a few times on EVPs. Usually paired with Gwen."

"You think the two of them are linked?" The implications were staggering. She needed to document this. If a ghost gave her information she didn't already have, it would be proof of the highest order. Except how would she prove that she hadn't known about Bernie in advance?

"I'm not sure." Christie lowered her voice. "We have something more pressing to speak about. Specifically, your young man."

"Greg didn't mean to break the horse," Jessica began wearily.

"I'm not talking about the horse." Anger flashed briefly across Christie's features before they resettled into concern. "There's something unsettling about him. And it's grown darker since you left."

"These aren't exactly the best circumstances—" Jessica began but Christie cut her off.

"The spirits don't like him. I thought it might have been both of you, but ever since you've been back, I can tell it's him. They welcome you, but they fear him and want him to leave." Christie took Jessica's hand between her own. The gesture felt oddly welcome, a long absent maternal touch. "I know you don't want to believe it, but he's dangerous."

145

"It was an accident." Jessica touched her eye, feeling the tender bruise.

"There's no such things as accidents. At some subconscious level, he chose to strike out. I'm not saying he would do it deliberately, but it is somewhere on his list of options." Her hostess's gaze stripped away the complexity, leaving bare and simple facts.

Angry at Christie's assumptions, Jessica pulled her hand away. "It's on mine, too. If that thing ever comes back—"

"What thing? You mean the entity in the demon box?" Christie's eyes narrowed. "What would that have to do with Greg?"

Oh shit. Jessica stopped, her mouth still open. What could she possibly say that the other woman would believe?

Christie raised one eyebrow. "Please don't lie to me. Even if it's embarrassing or unbelievable, tell me the truth."

"It possessed him. He offered himself to save me." The words dropped out of Jessica's mouth like leaden weights. The whole story poured out of her while the night deepened and the moonlight shifted across the worn wood floors.

"I see." Christie stood up. "Tell me exactly what you did when you drove the creature back into the box."

"It had been sealed with wax before, but we didn't have any. Greg used duct tape, two

146

rolls. And I wrote protective symbols on top of them. Then we wrapped the whole thing up in a garbage bag and another roll of tape." Jessica shuddered, remembering the horrible greasy feel of the entity. "I couldn't sense it after the first few layers, but we didn't want to risk anything."

"What did you do with it after?"

"I dipped the whole package in purified wax and then Father Thomas took it to the church graveyard and buried it under a rowan tree." Rowan wood protected from evil and Father Thomas was a believer. "That's certainly thorough. Yet, perhaps not enough." Christie bit her lip before continuing. "If any piece of the entity managed to stay in Greg, it could explain the nightmares and the warnings I've been getting."

"What warnings?" Chills swept through Jessica. She couldn't believe Greg might still be tainted from the demon. It just wasn't possible… unless she was wrong.

Christie stared out the window. "Danger and darkness coming. Something terrible about to be unleashed on the world. An entity like the one you describe would certainly qualify. Particularly if it proves to be infectious."

"It was only for a few minutes. We drove it out and contained it," Jessica insisted.

"Evil etches itself on the psyche. Like acid eating a bowl. Your young man's been corrupted." Christie sounded as if she were reciting old lessons.

Corrupted. Greg's angry outbursts came back to her. Last week, his sister commented that he must be in love because he certainly wasn't acting like himself. But it was the same question: demon influence or the result of the trauma? "What can we do?"

"I don't know if the cleansing ritual we talked about will work. We'd need someone like your mother to be able to sense whether or not something is still inside of him—or if it's only residue." Christie's chest swelled and deflated in a massive sigh. "It's beyond my abilities."

And mine. If only Jessica had her mother's talents. However, there was a more pressing issue. "Right now, we need to focus on what Chuck told us. I need your help to open my senses again." *And then maybe I can help Greg, too.*

"But the demon—"

"It's been months. Another few hours won't make the difference for Greg, and it sounds like it might for Chuck and Bernie." The little boy had sounded desperate and scared, the memory tugging at Jessica's conscience. "I need to find out what he was trying to tell me."

"Perhaps hypnosis. I could put you in a receptive trance, and we could see if you could make contact," Christie offered. "I've done it before with tourists wanting a more direct experience."

Hypnosis would mean placing her trust in

this woman, something Jessica wasn't sure she was ready for. Then she remembered Chuck's frightened eyes. Any interpersonal conflict with Christie suddenly didn't matter. Chuck was a child who needed help. Jessica refused to let him down.

They took over one of the empty guest rooms. Jessica lay on the bed and tried to follow Christie's instructions, relaxing without tipping over into sleep.

"Take a deep breath, concentrating on the way your lungs and ribs expand to make room. Exhale, feeling the air push through your throat and nose in a steady stream." Christie's repetitive directions guided Jessica into a deep trance state. Although Jessica hadn't tried this since she'd been a teenager, she slipped surprisingly easily into the peculiar combination of alertness and passivity. Her mind detached from the distractions of her body and conscious thought.

"Let your mind expand as if you're throwing open its windows and doors," Christie prompted, and Jessica duly performed the visualization. But her mental house stayed empty and silent while Jessica hovered in limbo. She tried to remember what Chuck had looked like in her dream, then imagined reaching out to him.

Only silence replied.

"Let's try something different," Christie

said. "Remember when you saw Tommy at Greg's house. Picture that moment in your mind."

It was easy to pull up. The little boy, barely half her height, with thick blond hair curling around his head, wearing a green and yellow Superfriends T-shirt and bell bottom jeans. He'd smiled at her, showing a gap between his front teeth. She'd wrapped her arms around him, feeling a tingly pins-and-needles sensation in her arm where they overlapped. It hurt in a mild way, but she'd wanted to give him a hug before he vanished into the light. The little boy who'd stayed in his home for decades, invisible and unknown. He deserved to be held.

"Remember how it felt to see him, to hear him," said Christie.

Jessica had been struggling so hard to sense him, to understand the darkness seeping through Greg's parents' home. She'd finished cleansing the house of spirits when something clicked into place in her mind, and she saw Tommy.

The cleansing. It created a safe place, a mental blank canvas which made it easier to see Tommy. Jessica opened her mouth, but it was like trying to speak after waking from a nightmare. Her throat simply wouldn't work.

"Easy now." She felt Christie's warm fingers rub gently along her throat. "You'll be able to speak now without breaking the trance."

"I need a cleansing circle," Jessica rasped.
"All right, one moment." The chair scraped
against the floor. Jessica heard drawers opening
and closing. Then she inhaled the smoky
sweetness of burning cedar and heard Christie's
voice moving around her, whispering too low to
make out the words.

With each pass, it was as if layers
of buzzing static were being eliminated
from Jessica's mind, layers she'd become so
accustomed to that she could only realize they'd
been there when they vanished.

"We ain't got time for this!" Chuck's voice
came through the distorting buzz, like an EVP.

"Chuck?" Jessica whispered.

"I got Bernie and her mom out, but they're
looking for them. The others can't get to
them in time. You have to help her." Chuck's
indiscriminate use of pronouns wasn't helping,
and Jessica struggled to understand.

"Who's looking for them?"

"The same men who took Shawna. They
grabbed her right off the street, shoved her
into a big black van. I went right to Bernie and
told 'em to run." Chuck straightened, obviously
proud of his accomplishments.

"Where are Bernie and her mother now?"
Jessica said carefully. Using words felt awkward,
like speaking in a foreign language.

"They're in a restaurant, one of those all-
night places, but the people there are gonna get

151

suspicious soon."

"What's the name?" Jessica asked. "Um, I don't read so good. I gotta check with Bernie." He vanished.

Jessica continued to breathe slowly and evenly, aware of the hiss of the wind outside and the warming cotton of the bedspread under her fingertips. She felt embedded in the world, an integral part of it rather than separate.

Chuck's reappearance didn't startle her. It felt inevitable and predictable. He excitedly passed on his information. "It's a Denny's. Near the highway, exit 37."

"Tell Bernie and her mother that we're on our way."

"I can't believe I'm driving to a meeting set up by a ghost." Greg pulled into the brightly lit parking lot. Only a few other worn trucks waited wearily on the faded asphalt, taking a brief break from the highway. Jessica got out of the car without saying anything, not even offering an arch look at his comment. She hadn't really spoken a word to him since she and Christie knocked on his door to tell him where they needed to go. Staring down her nose at him, Christie made Greg feel like a rotting piece of garbage. But what really hurt was wondering

152

if Jessica felt the same way. He should have been glad that she was keeping her distance; it meant he couldn't hurt her. But he hadn't expected to feel so alone.

He pushed open the glass door papered with children's menu artwork and scanned the restaurant. His nerves felt as if they'd been sanded, leaving them raw and exposed. Was the biker in the back paying too much attention to them? What about the couple staring blearily into their coffee cups? Were they trying to watch him and Jessica without being obvious? His head ached. *I'm a contractor, not a bodyguard. This is not in my training or skillset.*

"There they are." Jessica discreetly pointed out the mother and daughter sitting in a back-corner booth, picking at what remained of their toast and eggs. The preteen girl cheerfully hummed to herself while she stared at something near the ceiling. The exhausted mother's sandy blond hair straggled into her face, and a too-thin hand propped up her cheek.

The girl's eyes suddenly snapped to the couple approaching them, and a delighted grin lit up her face. She bounded out of the booth, running to Jessica with the enthusiasm of seeing a beloved aunt. "I knew you'd come!"

Greg turned his attention back to the mother, who had half risen, hand clutched to her collar in terror. The little girl led Jessica back to the table, tugging her by the hand and chattering nonstop.

"Hi. I'm Jessica and this is Greg."

"Martha. And Bernie," the mother replied, her fingers twitching as if she longed to snatch her daughter back to safety.

Bernie chattered on, oblivious to the tension. "Chuck said you were coming. It's been really exciting. We were waiting at the library, and he told us to hide in a back room. And then these men came—"

"That's enough, Bernie," Martha gently interrupted.

"We'll get you out of here, ma'am." The words were awkward on Greg's tongue. He eyeballed their meal and pulled out a couple of bills from his wallet. "We should get out of here as quickly."

"Hold on. First I'd like some confirmation that you are who you say you are." Martha's pale eyes stared at them like that of a cornered animal deciding whether to run or attack.

Bernie rolled her eyes. "Chuck says it's them."

"Chuck doesn't always think things through." Parental advice delivered, Martha focused again on Greg and Jessica. "Where are you taking us?"

"A bed and breakfast called Rose on the Grave. We were doing an investigation there when Chuck got in contact with us." Jessica looked up at Greg, a strange expression flitting across her face.

"We've called for friends to come and pick us up." Martha slowly got to her feet, clutching a heavy tote bag.

"Mom, we don't have time to wait. It'll be okay, I promise." The brief moment of maturity quickly passed. "Chuck said you have a truck. I've never ridden in a truck."

Greg and Martha followed Jessica and Bernie back out to the parking lot. Jessica and the girl managed to pull off something resembling normalcy but only if someone wasn't listening particularly hard. He and Martha looked like the token civilians in a spy film, too far out of their comfort zone to pretend to be cool. The eyes of the customers and staff seemed to follow him, making him want to turn around and lash out. *Sure, because that would be the smart move.* But he couldn't reason away the sensation of being hunted. He hurried everyone into the truck and drove out of the lot once they were all buckled in.

"Chuck says they'll be there in about twenty minutes," Bernie announced.

Greg was pretty sure he would get very tired of the phrase *Chuck says* before too much longer. "We won't be waiting around to see if Chuck is right."

"Agreed." Martha folded her lips grimly. "There have been too many close calls already."

Bernie cuddled up against Jessica in the

rear seat, watching the lights stream past the side window. Martha sat beside Greg in the front, her attention divided between the road and her daughter. "You said you were doing an investigation. Are you police?"

"No. Paranormal investigators. We call ourselves Spirit Sight, and we document hauntings," Jessica answered.

Martha barked out a rough laugh before covering her hand with her mouth. "I should have guessed. It seems everyone knew about ghosts but me."

"Shawna knows lots of really neat stuff. She used to listen to ghosts and people paid her money. She said I might be able to make money doing it when I'm grown up." Bernie poked her index finger at the glass as if testing whether or not it was real.

"Who's Shawna?" Greg asked, wondering if they needed to go back for another rescue.

"She was helping Bernie with her abilities—" Martha began.

"They took her right off the street this afternoon," said Bernie. "They were going to take us, too, but we listened to Chuck and crept out the back stairs."

The essential innocence of Bernie's ghoulish eagerness to relay such details left Greg feeling out of plumb. He kept checking the rearview mirror for any flashing lights signaling they'd been caught. *Who was after them?* If they found the mother and daughter, were their pursuers the type to leave corpses instead of witnesses? An image of Jessica lying in the street forced itself into his mental reel, blood pooling around her and eyes staring sightlessly at the sky. *Over my damn dead body.*

"Greg? Are you okay? Do you need me to drive?" Jessica's soft inquiry cut through the brooding build up.

"I'm fine." Whatever it takes, I will keep her safe. That was a contract, and he'd never broken a contract in his life. She would be better off without him, even if it left him with a gaping hole in his heart.

Jessica woke up in the dimness of their room at Rose on the Grave. From the sunlight edging the room-darkening blinds, it was just after dawn. Greg still slept beside her, the stress lines around his mouth finally relaxing. She eased out of bed without waking him. He needed all the uninterrupted sleep he could get. It could only help his temper.

Once he's awake, we can figure out how to help him. He'd been so quiet and withdrawn during their return trip. She'd wanted to tell him about the cleansing ritual but hadn't wanted to bring it up in front of Bernie and Martha. If Christie's exercises had helped Jessica to communicate with Chuck, then they should be able to help her see what was going on with Greg.

She dressed quickly in the dark and made her way down the hall to the church. Voices bounced down the hallway, chattering excitedly. So, she wasn't surprised to see Christie and Bernie talking together over the remains of a massive breakfast.

"Hi, Jessica!" Bernie chirped brightly. "Christie's taking care of me while Mom has a rest."

"That's nice. It looks like you were hungry." Jessica poured herself a cup of coffee from the carafe on the table.

"Christie makes really good pancakes. With chocolate chips in them special for me." Dark smears around Bernie's wide mouth attested to her enthusiasm.

"Anything left?" Jessica asked hopefully.

Christie smiled, rising from the table. "I'm sure I can dig something up."

"Thank you," Bernie said in a sing-song voice.

"How are you feeling this morning?" Jessica asked.

"Pretty good. Chuck said no one followed us. They still think we're near where our old home was."

The girl's matter of fact acceptance of people chasing her left Jessica feeling bruised. A

158

child shouldn't have to worry about such things. "It's a good thing that you have a friend like Chuck."

"I have a lot of ghost friends, but Chuck is my especial-favorite-best-friend. He helps me talk with Gwen, and she gives me lots of good advice. She talks kind of funny, and sometimes it's hard to figure out what she means, but she's really nice." Bernie grabbed her napkin. "Do you think Christie would make me some more pancakes if I asked really nicely?"

"I'm sure she would," Jessica said automatically, her brain still focused on the first half of Bernie's ramble. "Who's Gwen?"

"She's like me. She talks to ghosts. They talk to her all the time, and she doesn't like it, but she doesn't mind if Chuck and I talk to her." Bernie jumped up. "I better go ask Christie while she's still in the kitchen. Do you want pancakes?"

"Okay." Jessica nodded. Was Gwen real? She wanted to believe Bernie, yet the girl often seemed to be confused about what was real and what wasn't. She'd rambled in the car about a white knight who'd risen out of the flames to save her, and his girlfriend who could rip guns apart with her bare hands. Could Gwen be another spirit like Chuck? Or could she actually be a medium of some kind?

They talk to her all the time. Jessica wondered what that would be like. Even her mother had to make an effort to connect to the other side, and it wasn't reliable. Not like the clear communication that Bernie evidently heard. If she hadn't obtained information directly from Chuck, Jessica would have assumed the little girl was delusional. The dead simply didn't communicate so clearly with the living. Now her worldview was a little shakier.

The door to the kitchen opened, breaking her train of thought. Jessica hastily put a smile on her face to avoid upsetting Bernie, who skipped out hand-in-hand with Christie.

"Christie put away all the pancake stuff, but she said she'll make me some more later."

Bernie's grin suggested she wasn't upset at having to wait. "She asked me to talk to the ghosts here."

The request seemed harmless enough, even though a twinge of uncertainty resonated through Jessica. It seemed fundamentally wrong to ask a child to perform this kind of work, but Bernie's communication with the other side seemed effortless. It couldn't really hurt her and at worst, it would keep Bernie occupied for a while, giving her mother a much-needed break. She followed Christie and Bernie to the schoolroom.

Bernie dropped to her knees in front of the rocking horse, petting its peeling nose and exclaiming over the missing plug in its flank. She seemed so much younger than Jessica would have guessed from her size. *Maybe she's big for her age?* Her mother always said mediums came across as older than their years because of their psychic experiences. Only Jessica didn't think her mother ever came across someone with Bernie's powers.

"Do you see anyone, Bernie?" Christie asked, her hands clasped together like someone expecting the perfect Christmas gift.

Bernie didn't reply, running her fingers through the remnants of the stiff horsehair mane.

Christie smiled like one of the saints from the glass windows in the nave, but the picture of graceful indulgence struck a false chord with Jessica. She moved closer to Bernie, angling herself so that she could step between the little girl and their hostess if necessary.

"Bernie, darling, I need you to speak to the children here. I need to know if they're happy with what I've done." A hint of the whip surfaced beneath Christie's smoothness.

Bernie still didn't answer, playing with the horse, and irritation warped the beatific expression on Christie's face.

Jessica knelt beside the little girl and touched her arm. Bernie looked up, her eyes innocent and curious. Completely oblivious to Christie's growing frustration, the little girl waited for someone to speak.

"Do you sense anyone here?" Jessica asked,

161

keeping Bernie's attention focused on her. She didn't want the child to notice Christie until the woman composed herself.

"Not really." Bernie shrugged. "There's a white lady in the graveyard, but she's not really here. Just an echo. There's a grumpy man walking on the road outside, waving his stick. And Chuck, over there in the corner." She pointed at the empty desk in the far corner of the room.

"What about the children?" Christie interrupted.

"There aren't any kids here." Bernie's matter-of-fact reply left no doubt that she was more interested in getting back to whatever game she'd been playing with the horse.

"There must be children here. They were trapped in the fire." Christie insisted, eerily calm.

"I don't think so." Bernie shook her head, frowning as if the woman had claimed the sky was crimson red.

"Greg looked at the town newspaper. There was no mention of a fire." Jessica stepped between the little girl and an increasingly unhappy Christie.

"You can't trust what he says." Christie leaned around Jessica's attempts to block her. "Little girl, there have to be children here. I've heard from them. I've sensed them."

"Chuck says there were a lot of sick people in the graveyard. Maybe that's who you heard.

But they're all gone now. Whooshed up into the light." Bernie made rocket noises and zoomed her hand up to the ceiling.

"She's making a mistake." Christie's smile tightened in suspicion. "I know the children are here."

The ball in the corner suddenly rolled towards them. The tightness in Christie's smile relaxed, brightening with authenticity. "There, you see."

"That wasn't a ghost." Bernie's nose wrinkled upward in confusion.

"Sweetheart, just because you can't see it doesn't mean it isn't there. We all have different levels of sensitivity, and the children must be vibrating at a different frequency than you're attuned to."

Bullshit. Christie's explanation was pure garbage. The woman was grasping at straws and spewing whatever plausible nonsense occurred to her. Jessica wasn't sure how to defuse the situation. From Christie's whitened fists, she was having trouble accepting the truth.

"What's going on here?" Martha, Bernie's mother, appeared in the doorway, wet hair tied in a braid down her back.

"We were only having a bit of a look. It's a shame Bernie isn't sensitive enough." Christie regained her hostess's serenity by the edges of her fingernails.

Anger chilled Martha's expressions to

glacier levels. "You brought my daughter to speak to ghosts without even talking to me? You took advantage of her being alone?"

Jessica winced at the sudden onslaught of guilt. She hadn't even considered going to get Martha, even though it was the obvious choice in hindsight.

"There's no need to be upset. You shouldn't try to suppress your daughter's talent simply because you don't believe." Christie's nose lifted in the air and Jessica took a deep breath, her hands wrapped firmly around Bernie's shoulders. The little girl looked confused and frightened.

"This has nothing to do with what I do or do not believe. This is about you exploiting a naïve child for your own curiosity." Martha laid down each word with the precision of a judge passing sentence.

"I'm sorry, Mommy. I didn't know it was wrong." Bernie got to her feet, head hanging low. Jessica stood with her, still ready to defend the child if necessary.

Martha's voice softened immediately, and she held her arms out to her daughter. "You didn't do anything wrong, Bernie."

Bernie ran to her mother, wrapping her arms around the woman's waist and pressing her face to Martha's chest. "I didn't even see anything. She said maybe I'm broken."

Jessica's heart broke at the hurt in the little

girl's voice. Without understanding how or why, Bernie still knew she'd disappointed someone.

The look that Martha shot at Christie could have impaled a charging rhino. "You're not broken, honey. If there isn't anything to see, then there's nothing to see."

Christie lost the remnants of her control, hissing. "I have shelves full of documented sightings and events."

"I don't really care what you think you have. You will not be exploiting my daughter again." Martha turned to leave the room, guiding Bernie to walk with her.

Jessica tried to defuse the tension. "I think we all need to calm down."

Too bad Christie didn't feel a need to make the same effort. "You came to me for help, for a place to hide!"

"What's going on here?" Greg interrupted, still in his rumpled clothes and rubbing sleep from his eyes.

Disaster. That's what's going on. Jessica couldn't even begin to sum it up. Things couldn't possibly get any worse unless the people chasing Martha and Bernie started knocking on the door.

Bernie squinted up at Greg. "Did you know that there was a bad spirit living in you?"

165

The shouting only made Greg's pulsing headache worse. Christie was demanding that he leave the Rose immediately. Jessica was defending him. Martha was protecting her little girl in full mama-bear mode, and Bernie was shrilly demanding to be allowed to play with the horse some more.

"Enough!" He barked out, loud enough to make himself wince.

It worked though. The women stopped. Christie sniffed "If he's possessed, no wonder the children are hiding."

"He's not possessed." Jessica's hand tightened on his shoulder.

"You can barely sense the other side. You have no idea if something was left behind," Christie snapped back.

Hearing their hostess voice his inner fears made them even more terrifying. "She's right, Jess. It explains the nightmares, how easily I get angry since it happened. There's something wrong with me."

"There's nothing wrong with you," Jessica insisted, the love in her eyes making Greg wish he didn't have to disappoint her. "And even if there are some lingering traces, we can purge them."

"We can't risk it. If that thing is still inside of me— " He couldn't even say the words. He'd be better off pointing his car at solid wall than allowing the entity from the box to keep

166

growing.

"Hold on, here." Martha held up her hand before touching Bernie's chin. "Bernie, what exactly do you see in Greg?"

"It's kind of like an extra shadow. Like he needs another bath." Bernie frowned. "His light's all smudgy."

Greg's heart sank. He began frantically scanning the room. "You have to tie me up or lock me up somewhere."

"Greg—" Jessica's voice tried to catch his attention, but he didn't have time to waste. Once that thing realized its cover was broken, it would rise up and take over again. He needed to make sure he couldn't hurt anyone before it happened. He couldn't live with himself if he hurt Jessica or Martha or Bernie, or even Christie.

"Get the duct tape from the truck." It wouldn't be perfect but enough of it would hold him down.

"Quack, quack." Bernie giggled. "He's funny."

"Greg!" Jessica shouted, grabbing his shoulder.

He grasped her arms tightly. "Jessica, I love you. Please, I'm begging you. I'd rather die than hurt you. There's no time to waste."

"Greg, listen to me. The demon isn't inside you anymore. I'm sure of it." Jessica curled her hands around to grasp his wrists. "If it was, it would have acted before now."

"How can you be sure? I did that." His voice broke and trembling fingers twitched toward the fading remnants of the bruise circling her left eye.

"You were half awake and fighting a nightmare, not under a demonic possession," Jessica insisted.

"Bernie, is the bad spirit still inside the man?" Christie asked slowly.

Martha's lips tightened, but she didn't stop her daughter from answering. Bernie tilted her head from one side to the other, causing her fuzzy mass of hair to rock.

"Is there a bad spirit?" Martha asked.

"No. Just smudgy stuff. He really needs a bath." Bernie pronounced, pinching her nose in dramatic emphasis. Greg wanted to believe her. Wanted to believe the nightmare was over.

"It's making him all twitchy inside, like how sand gets in your bathing suit at the beach. I hate that!" The little girl stuck out her tongue in disgust.

"How do you wash a soul?" Jessica whispered, her beautiful brown eyes full of tears. Tears for him, which made him feel even worse.

"I…I know how. The cleansing I mentioned before." Christie hesitated. "A saltwater bath in a purification circle. Your mother and I used to do that with family heirlooms to cleanse them of their ghostly connections."

It didn't take long to collect the necessary ingredients. Christie apparently owned a massive container of purified sea salt that she used to keep unfriendly ghosts from invading the Rose. Their suite already had a massive Jacuzzi tub.

"Take everything off and put it in here," Christie ordered, proffering a rubberized bin. "It will insulate any negative influence from your clothing. If necessary, we'll burn it."

"Are you sure?" Jessica asked. Her faith in Christie had obviously fallen at some point before Greg woke up.

"I've been keeping out hostile ghosts for decades. I know what I'm doing." Christie folded her arms and watched him expectantly.

Greg felt a warm rush of blood creeping up his face. "I'm not really a 'strip in front of strangers' kind of guy."

Christie rolled her eyes. "Fine. I'll finish getting the bath ready. Once he's naked, he should go directly to the tub. I'll leave a gap in the circle of salt. You can close it once he's inside the circle."

"What happens after that?" Jessica's hand crept around his.

"He'll get into the water, making sure to immerse every part of him. Once he's cleansed, have him rinse off in the shower."

"Is that part of the ritual?" Greg asked. "No, I don't want salt-water dripped on my carpets." The humor only lightened Christie's eyes for a few seconds. Then her serious face returned. "Banish whatever is lingering in you. It's not part of you and shouldn't be allowed to hang about."

"It's probably harder than it sounds, isn't it?" Greg was tired of hand-wavy hippie-dippie claptrap. He wanted specific instructions this time.

"It is. You'll have to let go of your guilt. Accept that you were a victim, not in control of what happened to you. It's difficult for most men." Christie eyed Jessica. "Not too many people have to deal with the aftermath of possession. There aren't many survivors."

"Um, what about my clothes and stuff? Are going to have to burn them or something?" Greg asked. The thought of his painstakingly assembled tools being dunked in a tank of salt-water made him wince. He'd lose them all to rust. But it beat being haunted by more lingering demonic remnants.

"No, that won't be necessary. Once we cleanse you, the demonic essence will be gone unless you invite it back."

Christie sounded as if she thought he'd already scribbled a date in his calendar. Were people really stupid enough to keep invoking nasty spirits back into them?

Jessica caught the other woman's gaze. "Thank you, Christie." The three words were equal parts dismissal and gratitude.

Greg watched Christie suspiciously, expecting her to explode or huff in irritation.

"Your mother never accepted her limitations. Don't be a hero. If this doesn't work—"

"It'll work," Jessica insisted, firmly escorting Christie from the room. "I know it."

The door clicked shut, and Jessica twisted the lock closed. Greg looked at the roiling waters in the Jacuzzi. The salt crystals had vanished, dissolved into the maelstrom. "Guess it's time to start stripping down."

"I've never been opposed to that suggestion." Jessica leaning against the counter, putting on a brave face. Except Greg could see the tremors in her fingers.

He took her hands in his. "However this turns out, don't beat yourself up."

"I shouldn't have tried to take on a demon box by myself," she whispered.

"It didn't really give us much of a choice." The damned thing had sprung to life seconds after Jessica had helped the ghost-child Tommy move on.

"I knew the presence was darker than I'd seen before. I should have realized what that meant." Tears pricked those beautiful brown eyes. "Can you ever forgive me?"

"There's nothing to forgive." He kissed her, savoring the sweet softness of her willing mouth. He used to scoff at his married friends who told him that kissing their wives wasn't like kissing any other girl. *A kiss is a kiss. Mashing lips and tonsil hockey*, he'd thought. They'd shaken their heads, a pitying and secretive gleam in their eyes.

Now he understood. No one's lips tasted like Jessica's, or moved under his with soft mini-exhales, or warmed under his touch. No other kiss could ever compare to hers, and he couldn't imagine ever being interested in testing his conclusion. It was a simple fact, like the sunrise. She was his, and he was hers.

Which meant he really needed to get rid of whatever was staining his soul, so he could go back to being the man she deserved.

He broke the kiss and began shucking off his clothes, careful not to disturb the ring of white crystals surrounding the sunken tub.

Jessica collected his things, her face looking just as determined as he felt. Greg stepped into the warm waters, and she poured a fresh line of salt to seal the circle.

The water tugged and tickled, swirling around his legs. Taking a deep breath, he lowered himself into the tub, sinking down to sit in deep end. The miniature waves lapped at his neck and his arms floated just below the uneven surface. He'd been in hot tubs before, but this felt different. Like the water was snatching at him, trying to pluck something from beneath the surface of his skin.

"Ready?" Jessica asked.

Greg nodded. "I want this thing gone. I never wanted it in the first place, and I want it out now."

Clamping his lips together, he slid down under the water. With his eyes closed, the constant movement from the jets was disorienting. Some primal portion of his brain began shrieking that he could get tumbled around and lose track of which way was up, even though he was sitting on the firm ceramic base. He held his breath, letting the water scour him. It had to wash away the darkness. He wouldn't consider any other option.

Eventually, the need for oxygen forced him upwards. He didn't feel spiritually cleaner, but he still asked Jessica hopefully, "Did you see anything?"

She shook her head. "You were darker under the water than you should have been, like you were sitting in a shadow even though there's plenty of light here."

"Damn," he shook his head to send the water droplets clinging to his face flying.

"Maybe it's the denial part. She said you needed to stop blaming yourself." Jessica knelt on the tiled floor.

"I hurt you." Water popped out between his fingers as his fists clenched.

"It was an accident. Like the box." Her quiet words should have been soothing but they only scraped on his conscience like sandpaper. "I invited the damn thing in. To save you."

"That doesn't make you responsible for what it did. It only makes you brave. A little reckless, but mostly brave." She smiled at him, the trust in it sexier than any pin-up vixen's baring of teeth.

"I want it gone so that we can get back to living our lives. You hear me, whatever you are, time to vacate!" He took another deep breath and plunged himself under.

This time he felt it, a zinging electrical current skimming the surface of his skin along with the plucking water. It scoured him, and he finally began to feel clean again. The tainted darkness was being scrubbed and banished, swirling away from him to dissolve into the salt-laden fluid.

He burst up, grinning at the exhilaration. Jessica grabbed at his outstretched arms, reaching over the containing circle.

"It worked!" Excitement shone in her eyes. "The shadow is gone."

He pulled her close, driving his mouth into hers in triumph. He didn't care about the water sheeting off him and soaking into her clothes.

The sweet taste of her mouth drove him wild, and he planted his feet to rise up, wanting to feel her against him.

She moaned against his kiss. "Don't break the circle."

Right. That had been one of Christie's instructions. He carefully stepped over the binding ring, then gave himself up to the raw hunger coursing through his veins. He stripped away Jessica's shirt, baring the dark lacy bra cupping the perfect swell of her breasts. Growling in appreciation, he began to taste his way down her chest. Sweet wholesome honey, that was his girl's flavor, and he could lick up every last drop.

Jessica's powers of rational thought had gone on a most welcome vacation with Greg crouched in front of her, his tongue and lips moving over her flesh like a tattooing gun. She clung to his broad shoulders as she leaned against the counter, incredibly turned on by the reality of having his potent masculine power focused entirely on her. She'd literally brought him to his knees as he worshipped her. Her head tilted back as he gripped her hips to thoroughly employ his eager mouth. Of course, turnabout was fair play, and the idea of getting to do the same sent a jolt of excitement through her. Her knees decided to veto any further semblance of control and buckled.

He supported her easily with his powerful

arms, holding her at the perfect height and angle so that he could tease her tightened nipple through her bra. He always liked playing with her breasts, coaxing sensations she'd never thought could come from them. Sometimes he liked to set himself the challenge of making her orgasm purely through such play. They would lie in bed and he would tease with his mouth and fingers until she screamed in delight.

Today he was more intent, and Jessica wholeheartedly supported his agenda. He lifted her up, staggering to his feet. She buried her hands in his slick wet hair, and he took her mouth again, kissing her as if they'd been separated for years.

Her legs wrapped around his waist, and he braced her against the counter top. A brief moment of reality intruded. Not wanting a structural failure to ruin the moment, she panted. "Is this okay?"

"It's Juperana granite. It'll hold." He grinned devilishly. "Trust me."

"You're the contractor." She grinned back, running her hands over his delightfully thick muscles.

"I think there might be a little work we have to do here, though." He slid his hand down her belly, dipping his fingers behind the waistband of her jeans.

Jessica's channel clenched and flexed in aching anticipation. "I hope nothing serious."

"I won't know until I get in there and have a look, ma'am." His hand flattened, sliding lower to finger the first guardian curls.

Delicious tension began to build as she felt him edging closer. "By all means." She

half-closed her eyes, arching her back to give him more room.

He touched the swollen readiness of her clit and flicked it gently with his fingertip. "I think I found the issue."

She couldn't play the game anymore when he began to fondle her. She gasped and clung to him, riding and shuddering against his clever fingers.

"Looks like it needs some attention," he whispered against her neck, popping the button on her jeans.

"Whatever you say." She lifted herself up, letting him strip away the remaining layers of clothing.

"That's my girl." He slid himself into her welcoming folds, and both of them surrendered to the moment. Sweat slick skin clung together as tightly as their arms and legs. He began to pump against her, each thrusting drive sending her higher and higher.

Everything dissolved into a splendid thrum of ecstasy. He cried out her name, and she might have done the same, but nothing existed outside the union of their flesh and spirit. They were one, indivisible and united, just as they'd always been meant to be.

"All better now," Bernie sang out when Jessica and Greg emerged into dining area. Her drawings were scattered over the table, and she was busily squeaking a marker over a new one with careless disregard for Christie's immaculate tablecloths. Her mother sat nearby, an uneaten sandwich on a plate in front of her. Greg's stomach rumbled to life.

Martha pushed the sandwich toward him. "Go ahead. I'm not hungry but I remember how upending my entire life stimulated the appetite."

Greg accepted the ham and cheese gratefully, tucking in without another word.

"Bernie tells us that our friends should be here shortly." Martha smoothed her daughter's unruly curls with one hand. "The people looking for us have realized we somehow escaped, so we'll have to move quickly."

"I'm sorry. I wish I could do more to help." Jessica sat down beside Greg.

"With all the changes happening, I wonder if anywhere will be safe." Martha stared at the stained-glass windows. "I'm afraid of what will happen next."

"You don't have to be scared, Mommy. It'll

all work out." Bernie dropped her markers and wrapped her arms around her mother.

"Of course, Bernie-Bear." Martha held her daughter.

Greg saw the uncertainty in the mother's eyes.

"Do you want to go play with the horse again?" she added.

Bernie jumped up and started to head for the schoolroom before hesitating and running to Greg. "I'm glad you're all bright and shiny again. It looks much better on you."

"Thanks." *I think*. He couldn't help smiling at the girl bouncing her way to the schoolroom. She was such an odd mixture of innocence and knowledge. The three adults waited until she was safely out of earshot before continuing.

"Where's Christie?" Greg asked. Her ritual had worked, and he owed her an apology.

"Out in the garden, thinking. She was fairly upset about what Bernie told her." Martha's lips tightened briefly.

"Someone should warn her about what's coming." Jessica rose to her feet and stopped. Christie appeared in the doorway between the dining area and the lobby.

The hostess studied Greg carefully. "I wasn't sure the cleansing would work."

"I feel like myself again. Thank you." Greg kept his distance, not wanting to push matters.

"That makes one of us." Christie's sad eyes

turned to Jessica. "According to Bernie, there used to be some child spirits here, but they've been gone for some time. Soon after I finished the renovations."

"What about the moving toys? And the EVPs?" Jessica asked.

Martha cleared her throat softly. "Christie may be telekinetic, able to move things with her mind. I've seen it before, with a young man at a safehouse we were hiding at."

"A telekinetic. That's got to be something of a surprise." Greg sat down across from Christie, who steepled her fingers, resting them against her forehead.

"I thought I was opening my senses to ghosts, but maybe I trained something else in my mind. Perhaps this is a strange thing to say for someone who believes in ghosts, but the idea of telekinesis seems impossible." Christie gave a weary chuckle.

Martha smiled gently, mother to mother. "It would be nice if the world could go back to clear boundaries between what's real and what isn't. But I've learned that what is impossible is more of a suggestion than a certainty these days. All I know is I have to keep Bernie and her skills hidden."

"Why? She could help so much with paranormal investigations and how to figure out which hauntings are real or faked. When she's older, of course." Jessica turned to look toward the schoolroom and the cheerful monologue echoing from inside.

"You have to understand. Six months ago, I thought she was delusional." Martha stared at the schoolroom wall as if she could see right through it to keep a protective eye on her daughter. "Doctors told me she was hallucinating."

"But it was ghosts." Greg couldn't imagine having to go through that. To spend years believing a child was crazy and then to learn they were actually telling the truth about what they saw and heard—that there was a reason for it.

"It was ghosts." Martha agreed with a sigh. "Unfortunately, we found out because a very dangerous man took Bernie in order to use her abilities. I got her back, and we've been on the run ever since."

"We're all going to have to be on the run now." Christie pushed herself back from the table, leaning back on her chair in a display of restlessness.

Jessica's hand crept into Greg's under the table, seeking comfort. He wrapped his fingers around hers. If someone came after her, he wouldn't let anyone take her.

"With the President's announcement, there will be more people wanting to hunt for those like Bernie and the two of you. They'll want to use your abilities or resent that you have them."

Martha's chin lifted, ready to fight. "The only way I can keep her safe is if they don't know where she is."

"She's right. The best way to keep from being caught is for no one to be here when they arrive." Christie stood up. "I'll pack up a few things and go."

"What about the Rose? You've worked so hard for this." Jessica rose and caught Christie by the arm. "You can't just walk away."

"There's nothing for me here anymore." Christie looked up at the stone walls and stained glass. "I only really wanted to be here to protect the children and instead, all I've been doing is tricking myself and effectively talking to myself."

"You helped us." Greg straightened.

"Without you, I would still be fighting the shadows in my mind."

Christie smiled but there was no disguising a broken heart. "I'm glad I could help you. But Martha is right. We need to run and hide if we don't want to end up hunted and trapped. I wish you both well."

She left and this time, Jessica let her go. She returned to Greg, tucking herself onto his lap and into his arms, pressing her forehead against his.

"Tough situation. For both of them." Greg held her, enjoying being able to do so without worrying about what lurked in his subconscious.

"I feel guilty about how happy I feel. There's so much going wrong in their lives, but I can't help being glad that you're back." Jessica kissed him softly on the cheek, letting her fingers trail down the side of his face. Greg wished they could head back to the room, but there was too much bearing down on them.

"That makes two of us."

"I should have asked for help sooner." Jessica ran her fingertips over his chest, the warmth tracing an enticing pattern through his thin cotton shirt.

"I don't think the Yellow Pages have a Demonic Possession section." Greg pulled her forward to rest his forehead against hers. "We got through this."

"What about next time?" Jessica clung to his shirt. "If I keep chasing ghosts, we could both end up hurt."

A chill went through him. "Are you thinking of giving it up?"

"I don't know enough to do it safely." Jessica drew back, wiping at her cheeks with the back of her hands. "I'm like those teenagers in a horror film reading the book of demon-summoning aloud just for fun."

"Hey, that's a little harsh. Although, if you wanted to be the hot girl who investigates in your lingerie, I might be able to go with that. Provided we only do private investigations." He hoped she would laugh.

No luck. "This isn't funny."

"It's also not the time to make major decisions. You're only beginning to learn how to use your powers. What happened to wanting to prove ghosts are real to show that your mom wasn't a complete fake?" He held her hands tightly, a terrifying feeling swirling in his stomach. He couldn't lose her, not after everything they'd gone through.

"I still want to do that. But someone like Bernie would be much better at it. I'm useless." She hung her head.

"Hey. No one insults my girl." He pulled her closer. "I would be lying if I said I wasn't scared. And not just about the demon stuff. There's all sorts of crap going down right now, and I don't want to find myself hiding you from some kind of paranormal police unit. But we can't make decisions out of fear."

She met his gaze again.

"You're going to keep learning to use your gifts. Everything else, we'll deal with it. You don't start a renovation without finding some surprises, and I know that we can tackle whatever pops out of the walls."

She leaned in, brushing her lips against his. "Together."

"Together," he promised.

THIRD EYE OPEN

#3 Spirit Sight

"I'm sorry to have to tell you that we didn't find any evidence of the supernatural in the apartment."

Jessica wished she'd taken the time for a second cup of coffee before sitting down to discuss the investigation results with their client. Gently removing someone's illusions was hard enough without managing a pounding headache from being awake for the last three nights.

Greg squeezed her hand under the kitchen table where their client wouldn't see.

"But there must be…" Penelope Laplante seemed bewildered, her thick lashes fluttering over her big blue eyes fast enough to strike up a stiff breeze. "What about the pictures falling off the walls? The cold spot in the kitchen? The weird laughter in the bedroom?"

"The pictures fell off the walls because the nails weren't long enough to support them. There's an HVAC duct running underneath the kitchen floor, and it's not well insulated. We were able to see it on FLIR, and I can give you those images for your landlord." Jessica clicked a picture of a blue rectangle surrounded by yellow.

Greg pointed at the rectangle. "The deeper the color, the colder the object and in this case, that duct is carrying the cold air for the air conditioners."

Penelope opened her mouth to argue further, but Jessica continued.

"I'm pretty sure the laughter is from your neighbor. She gets in from work between two and three in the morning and watches old sitcoms to unwind. She uses headphones to avoid disturbing everyone, but she does laugh out loud frequently." Stifling a yawn, Jessica hoped the woman would be satisfied.

"The air ducts between your rooms echo," Greg added.

"But the psychic said it was a ghost, a little child who'd been murdered." Penelope's narrow lips thinned further.

Because they always say they see a child, usually a little girl. Usually named Sarah. Jessica bit her own tongue before she could speak her uncharitable thoughts. She knew better than anyone else that there were genuine mediums and psychics in the world, but there were also a large number of fakes and scammers. Those with genuine abilities tended not to advertise their services. Jessica's mother had been an exception, using her abilities to launch a short-lived television show called *Spirit Sight: Conversations from the Grave*. However, she'd quickly discovered that even a genuine gift wasn't enough to keep up with the demands of a production schedule and began supplementing real readings with trickery. When she was caught, the family faced a lot of angry recriminations from former believers.

"Investigating psychic phenomena isn't an exact science." Greg offered Penelope an easy charm-laden smile.

Jessica's mouth twitched as Penelope's lashes fluttered even faster while her hand drifted up to touch her throat in a subconscious flirtatious gesture.

The client cooed, "I didn't mean to imply you were wrong. It's fascinating how differently everyone approaches these things. I'm sure you must have seen lots of exciting things, Mr. Cook."

"Only when I'm unlucky." Another finger-squeeze. "I know this wasn't what you were hoping for, but we can only report on what we find. And in the end, isn't it good news if there isn't a scared and unhappy child trapped in your apartment?"

This time Jessica didn't bother to hide her smile. Greg had come a long way from the man she'd met two years ago. Back then, he'd assumed she was a fraud, along with anyone who claimed to have seen a ghost. *Of course, those were the days before the world discovered psychic powers were real.*

"Maybe if you stayed another night?" Penelope's flirty hand floated to her plunging neckline. "If there is a little girl, maybe she'd be more comfortable coming out if I was there."

And now we're done. Jessica stood up. "I'm sorry to disappoint you, but there's no evidence of any supernatural activity. I'll send you a full report."

Leaving Penelope sputtering hopeful entreaties, Jessica and Greg left the apartment, blinking in the too-bright morning sunshine.

"Thanks for the save, O brave knight." Greg winked at her. "That not-so-innocent maiden was about five minutes from ravishing me. However might I thank you for protecting my virtue?"

She laughed, the mirth only slightly tinged with the exhaustion-drunkenness from not enough sleep. "How much time do we have before work?"

"Not enough for what I'd like." His words didn't stop him from planting a long, lingering kiss, which made her wonder if their respective bosses would actually fire them if they came in late again. From the smolder in his eyes, Greg was doing the same calculation.

"We'll have to save it as a promise for later," he added. "You've got to be at Billy's in fifteen minutes, and I've got to get to the site five minutes after that."

On mornings like this, she hated her job at Billy's Breakfast Bar, but it paid the bills and let her fund their ghost-hunting business. Greg contributed where he could, but an independent contractor's income was more precarious than hers, especially as the recession dragged on.

Jessica had named her paranormal investigation business *Spirit Sight*, after her mother. She didn't have her mother's gifts as a medium, but she wanted to find out the science that would allow people to distinguish real hauntings from the fakes. When the occulata came out of the closet last year, revealing that paranormal abilities were actually real, Jessica had been swamped with requests for information about ghosts and hauntings.

She'd done a few online videos explaining the more common haunting phenomena: manifestations, electronic-voice phenomena, electrical disturbances, and such. To her surprise, they'd become viral hits. In the last six months, Jessica went from posting flyers in new age stores to having a waitlist for clients. Unfortunately, not all of those clients wanted the truth. And the sheer volume of them was wreaking havoc on her daytime schedule.

She crawled into the passenger seat of the truck and buckled her seat belt. "I'm tired enough to fall asleep right here."

"You're pushing yourself too hard." The humor was gone from Greg's voice, replaced with worry.

"Maybe we should reconsider charging a token fee for the investigations."

"No." She glared at him, and he held up his hands in surrender.

"It wouldn't have to be much, and we could waive it if the client is having trouble." His face softened. "I'm worried about you. You've only gotten three hours of sleep in the last thirty-six hours and you've been pushing yourself for months."

"I know." Her brief show of irritation had drained what little energy she seemed to have left. "I hate making people wait when they need help."

"They'll wait a lot longer if you burn yourself out." He picked up her hand and kissed her fingertips. His voice took on the special throaty growl he used when they were making love. "I'm selfish enough to want my amazing girlfriend to be able to stay awake when she gets home in the morning."

She caressed his lips with her fingers. "I love you, too."

He dropped her off at the restaurant. She helped herself to a large coffee and managed to make it through her shift. When she finally clocked out in the early afternoon, Jessica decided to indulge in an Uber to get home. Even if her car was in the parking lot, she wouldn't have trusted herself to drive.

"Hey, you're the chick from the videos! *Spirit Sight*, right?" the young woman asked excitedly.

"Yes, that's me." Jessica managed a tired smile from the backseat.

"Nice to meet you. I'm Stephanie. I watch your videos all the time. My favorite is the one with the picture of the grandmother hovering over the baby's crib. That one makes me cry. It's so sweet to think of the people we love still taking care of us after they go." Stephanie grinned. "Say, wasn't your mom a famous medium, too? You two must have all kinds of talks."

"She passed away several years ago." Jessica rubbed at her eyes. Everything seemed far too raw today. "She's the one who inspired me to start investigating."

"Doesn't she still talk to you? I mean, wouldn't a medium be really good at being a ghost?"

It would be a lot easier if she did. An experience like that would eliminate all kinds of skepticism. And ease the fears that Jessica still harbored, wondering if her mother would have come to see the value of Jessica's work. "I'm afraid I haven't heard directly from her since her passing."

"I'm sorry to have asked." Stephanie lowered her eyes, abashed. "It wasn't any of my business."

"It's all right. I would have said if I didn't want to answer." Jessica hid a yawn behind her hand. "I miss her. But I'm glad she's not a ghost. Most of the ghosts I see are unhappy and scared. I wouldn't want that for my mom." *Even if it would be nice to talk to her again.*

"Good plan. Here we are." The car came to a halt in front of the apartment building. "Are you going to be okay to get upstairs?"

"I'll be fine. Thanks for the drive." Jessica entered a five-star review and made her way to her apartment. Greg would be at the construction site for a few more hours. There were any number of tasks she could have done, but none of them held the appeal of the still-unmade queen-sized bed. She crawled into the tangle of sheets and pillows, not bothering to get undressed.

It seemed like only a few seconds later she felt hands tugging at her jeans. Wearily she opened her eyes to see Greg leaning over her.

"Hey there," he whispered. His roguish smile still had the power to weaken her knees.

Jessica blinked. The apartment was much darker than it should have been.

"Come on. You'll regret it if you spend the night in your jeans and bra." His strong fingers undid the button at her waist and slid inside to ease the denim off her hips.

"What time is it?" Jessica yawned, trying to spot the clock.

"Past eight." He tugged her jeans down her legs.

Panic sent a punch of adrenaline to her internal wake-up button. "I was supposed to be at Mrs. Juniper's for seven."

"I called her and said you weren't feeling well." Greg caught her before she could stand up. "I told her we would reschedule."

"But when? We've got investigations scheduled every night for the next two weeks!" The idea of trying to fit it in made her slump in exhaustion.

"We'll figure something out. If worse comes to worse, we could split up, and I'll handle the investigation at Mrs. Juniper's. She's eighty years old with a dozen cats and hearing odd thumping noises. Odds are good of it not being an actual haunting." He leaned in and kissed her forehead. "She was very understanding and told me I should make sure you ate plenty of chicken soup."

The instructions sounded exactly like Mrs. Juniper, who had spent a lot more time wanting to know about Jessica's life than sharing the experiences that had prompted her to call a paranormal investigator. Some investigators would have dismissed the woman as wanting attention, but Jessica preferred not to make those kinds of judgments. *Even if she does want attention, it's a small kindness, and it makes her happier. And that made it worth* doing. She leaned back on the bed. "Sounds like Penelope hasn't been the only client flirting with you today."

"They can drool at the window all they want." Greg leaned over, brushing his lips over her cheeks and lips. "You're the only one who gets to come into the store. And right now, I'm more interested in celebrating your first evening off in three months."

Jessica ignored the part of her brain attempting to remind her of all the things she should take care of during this unexpected respite. Instead, she allowed herself to enjoy the warmth of Greg's arms around her and the reassuring rhythm of his heartbeat. Idly, she slipped her hand underneath his T-shirt to run her fingers along his muscled chest.

"Mmmmm." He grinned at her. "Need help getting back to sleep?"

"Maybe." She smiled coyly. "You're the one who started it by undressing me."

"Just trying to be a gentleman. My mother taught me to always make sure my girl was comfortable." He reached behind her back and unsnapped her bra.

"So, your actions are entirely altruistic." She squirmed closer, throwing her leg over his thighs.

"Absolutely. I would never dream of trying to take advantage of you in your sleep-deprived state." He shifted them, positioning her underneath him and leaning in for a long, slow kiss. His lips lingered on hers, as if savoring an anticipated treat.

She tugged at his shirt, eager to feel his skin against hers. He broke off the kiss and raised an eyebrow at her.

"Are you attempting to seduce me, ma'am?"

She grinned at him. "Is it working?"

He dipped his head for another long, fevered kiss.

"You tell me."

"Maybe I need to send a clearer message." She yanked off her top and loosened bra and was rewarded by an appreciative masculine inhale.

"I'm not one of those college-educated guys. I might need something more obvious." He stood up and stripped off his own clothing, revealing a spectacular body. *Forget the gym, nothing beats contractors.*

She loved how he could make her laugh and banish the looming darkness. Unpaid bills, deadlines, demanding clients, they all vanished when the two of them were together like this. "I'm naked in your bed. Seems like a pretty clear invitation to me but if you're not interested…"

He leaned down over her, his thick arms braced to either side. Their mouths met in a fiery, demanding mash of tongues and lips. She buried her fingers in his short hair and wrapped her legs around his waist, pulling him closer.

Her thin cotton panties were the only barrier between them, and she could feel his erection rubbing against her slick core.

His lips left hers, moving down her exposed skin. Nibbling kisses marked the trail from her neck, between her breasts, and along her belly. She sucked in a breath as he knelt between her parted thighs and tugged aside the fragile fabric.

Coherent thought left the building. His tongue and lips began to tease her clit. She moaned, clenching the rumpled blanket in her fists as he skillfully drove her toward orgasm. Bucking against him, she cried out at the ecstasy exploding throughout her body. Dimly, she was aware of a shift in position when he thrust into her, every strong stroke only prolonging the shuddering bliss.

"Hey, Cook. You look tired. Rough night chasing Casper?"

Greg ignored Bobby's crude taunt, focusing on properly smoothing plaster. He was tired enough that his whole body ached. He might have persuaded Jessica to take a break last week, but it seemed to have only driven up the pace. Last night's investigation had been at a motorcycle club's headquarters, and he'd been on high alert the entire time.

"Or maybe Casper was chasing you!" None of the rest of the crew laughed, but the lack of enthusiasm didn't stop Bobby from braying like he'd delivered the funniest joke since the road-crossing chicken.

"I have to say, if I got a chance to hang out in a dark house all night with that sweet piece of action, I'd pretend to believe in ghosts, too." Bobby stood close enough for Greg to smell the soured beer and onion on his breath.

It's not even nine thirty. Doesn't this guy ever brush his teeth? Concentrating on the man's poor oral hygiene let Greg avoid reacting to the insult to Jessica. Bobby was the nephew of the head contractor, and Greg needed to keep this job if they were going to pay their bills. Two more payment past due notices had been waiting in the mail this morning.

"Bobby," Manuel, the site manager, called out, "Go check the boxes of tile for the kitchen. I don't want to come up short halfway through this job."

Greg breathed a sigh of relief when Bobby stalked away. Maybe the jerk would find someone else to torment for the rest of the day.

"Is there going to be a problem?" Manuel stood only a few feet away.

Greg finished the installation and stood up. "Not on my end. I don't know why Bobby is determined to get a rise out of me, but I'm here to get my work done."

199

Manuel's chin shifted slightly, a bare hint of an approving nod. "I don't like trash talk on my site. It's not professional."

"Couldn't agree more." Greg collected his tools. "This room is done. I'll take care of the ones upstairs."

"I'll keep Bobby busy on the ground floor." Manuel tilted his head back. "You do good work. When this job is done, I've got some other jobs that I could use a good man on."

"I'm not about to say no to work." Greg shook the other man's hand, relief unknotting some of the tension in his neck. Before Jessica, he'd never been particularly concerned about potential gaps between work. He had a strong reputation, and jobs came in a reasonably steady stream. But in the last few months, he'd found himself compulsively checking the calendar and bank balance to make sure there was enough cash to stretch.

If only Jessica would start charging for the investigations. It didn't have to be much, but fifty or sixty dollars would help to start covering the gas and ghost-hunting equipment. His feet thunked hollowly with each plodding step up the stairs, hauling his bucket of drywall compound and his tools. *We can't keep going at this pace.*

But she hated the idea. He'd heard her complain about how accepting money made it a business transaction and increased the client's expectations. She felt payment would compromise her integrity, and he couldn't ask her to do that, especially not after what happened with her mother. *Still…I'm good at building houses and doing renovations. I enjoy it. Doesn't mean I ought to do it for free.*

His teeth scraped together, and he made himself relax his jaw before he gave himself a tension headache. Although he was nominally a partner in Spirit Sight, he'd always recognized this was Jessica's passion and primarily her business. He'd reined in his inherent drive to take care of things for her and be in control. But he couldn't help worrying with each arriving bill and how the hours in the day got shorter and shorter. *If she keeps up this pace, it's going to kill her.* She could get sick, have an accident in the car, or any number of scenarios that made his heart constrict in his chest.

As he smoothed the plaster over the seams in the drywall, a scratching sound filled the room. Frowning, he straightened. He'd been on sites before where wild animals got caught in the walls. *The drywall guys were supposed to check.* Except, it was coming from the other side of interior wall, from the room where the drywall team was currently working.

An irregular moaning started up, punctuated by stifled snickers.

Bobby. This was the sixth time the man had tried to make Greg jump. He knew exactly what was happening. Bobby was threatened by him and wanted to boost himself up by bringing Greg down. Since Greg wasn't reacting the way Bobby wanted, the other man was escalating his efforts. *Of course, if I did react, he'd get vicious and never let up.* There was no way for Greg to get what he wanted, which was to be left alone to do his work.

"I miss being able to walk away," he said quietly to himself. In the past, if he'd been stuck with a jerk like Bobby, he would have either quit or insisted on being moved to a different project. It was the beauty of being independent. He didn't have to put up with crap if he didn't want to.

It's only another six weeks. Eight at most. With luck, he'd get more jobs through Manuel. Ones that didn't involve jerks running their mouths out of a misplaced urge to bolster their pathetic masculinity.

Bobby's moaning was getting louder and louder. Greg kept working with gritted teeth, ignoring it. He could hear the guys on the drywall team muttering to the other man to give it up and get back to work.

Suddenly Manuel appeared in the hallway. "Bobby, is this a new career? Are you being paid to sing now?"

The moaning and scratching stopped. Greg kept his head down and concentrated on covering the seam in the drywall with perfectly smooth plaster.

"I'm on a break." Bobby's sullen voice came through the thin walls easily.

"Yes. You are. Permanently. Pack your things and leave my site." Manuel folded his arms.

"Come on. I'm just having a little fun. It's not my fault Cook is such a—"

"Pack your things and leave my site. You've gotten your last warning."

An experienced contractor would recognize the note of steel in Manuel's voice. *A professional would never have gotten caught up in this bullshit pissing contest to begin with.* But Bobby wasn't a professional. He was a kid who was coasting on his relationship to the boss.

Sure enough, that was Bobby's next tactic. "My uncle won't let you fire me!"

"Your uncle is more concerned with getting the work done than protecting your ego."

Manuel pointed. "Leave now, or I'll call the police to have you escorted away."

A series of muttered curses marked Bobby's exit, granting everyone a heaping helping of his abuse. As he sulked past the door, Bobby shot a glare of pure venom at Greg.

Great. He blames me. Greg sighed, pretending he couldn't hear the dwindling tirade or the mutters from the other room. Bobby's antics had garnered support from other bullies, and Greg hoped no one would pick up where Bobby left off.

His phone rang. He recognized his sister's number.

"Hey, Olive. What's up?"

"Are you busy right now?" she asked breathlessly. "Could you come meet me?"

One of the other workers poked his head into the room, his eyes suspicious with a hint of triumph.

Greg stayed steady, keeping his level gaze on Bobby's would-be avenger. "I can't talk now, Olive. I'm working."

If this is another request to "just look" at

something in her apartment, I'm going to be seriously pissed. His sister didn't share his conviction about being paid to work and seemed to think she was entitled to free repairs based on their shared DNA.

"We can go to him," a male voice in the background announced cheerfully.

"Who was that?" Greg demanded. "It's probably better if I tell you in person. Send me the address and we'll be there to take you to lunch."

Jessica put the freshly-inspected spare battery into its place. No one had quite figured out how or why, but electrical batteries often

204

went dead in areas with hauntings. Every professional paranormal investigator made sure to carry spares and to check them frequently. She glanced at the clock. It was two hours past the time when Greg would normally be home, and they were due at the Johnston's in another hour and a half. *It's not like him to not call.*

The phone rang. She snatched it without looking at the display. "Hello?"

"Jessica?" an older woman's shaken voice asked, punctuated by a loud sniff. "It's Ellie McFadden, from St. Michael's."

"Ellie? What's wrong?" Jessica sank down into a chair. Her mother had worshipped at St. Michael's, and Jessica had maintained close relationships with the staff. They believed in ghosts and had helped with a number of cleansings and exorcisms over the years.

"I wanted you to know before someone else told you. Father Thomas died last night." Ellie took a deep breath. "We've been having a problem with vandalism at the church and graveyard. We think he heard something and went out to investigate."

"Was he hurt?" The idea of someone attacking the elderly priest caused a stab of pain in Jessica's heart. Father Thomas had been one of the kindest, gentlest men she'd known—one of the rare genuinely selfless people.

"The police don't think so. They think he tried to run after them, but his heart couldn't take the strain. We found him this morning. They're saying it happened very quickly. He probably didn't even feel it."

"I'm so sorry, Ellie. Is there anything I can do to help?" She'd find the time somehow.

"Thank you, dear. He always spoke so highly of you and the work you did. For now, I don't think there's anything, but I'll let you know when the service is going to be."

After a few more minutes of chatting and sharing memories, she hung up and buried her face in her hands. Everything seemed to be collapsing at once. She was exhausted and overwhelmed. Greg was forced to work late at a job he hated to pay the bills.

As if her thought summoned him, the apartment door opened, and he stepped inside. Maybe it was the harsh light or her own harsh thoughts, but the dark circles under his eyes seemed heavier than they had before. The spring was gone from his step and his smile was a shadow of what it usually was. Father Thomas had given selflessly, and his body had given out. *The same thing could happen to Greg.* She threw herself at him, wrapping her arms around him.

"Hey," he said in surprise. His arms closed around her. "What's wrong?"

She told him about Father Thomas's death. "No!" He pulled back, his mouth gaping. "That the same priest who helped after the haunting at my parents' house, right?"

She nodded. "He used to help my mother, too, and he's exorcised any number of malevolent spirits. It just seems so wrong for him to have died alone."

His embrace tightened. "Maybe we should cancel tonight."

"I don't know." She wiped at the tears trickling down her cheeks. "On the one hand, part of me says Father Thomas dedicated his life to others. He would have wanted us to do the investigation. On the other hand, his death feels like a horrible warning to change what we've been doing, or else we could end up in our own graves."

He went very still. "Did Olive call you?"

"No." The mention of his sister threw Jessica for a moment. "Oh my God, did something happen to your parents?"

"They're fine," he reassured her. "Olive came to my job site today, along with Calvin Atherton.

The name sounded familiar, but Jessica couldn't place it.

"He said he's been trying to contact you for the last six weeks." Greg dropped into the couch, leaning his head back and stretching his feet out in front of him.

Her email. That's where she'd seen the name. But she still couldn't pull up any details about his case. "Is it a serious haunting?"

"It's not about a ghost. It's about you."

Greg rubbed his face with his hand. "Sorry, I'm not trying to be cryptic. I'm worn out and kind of in shock. I know the timing isn't great, but he's with one of the streaming networks, and he wants to do a show with you as one of the co-hosts."

Jessica swallowed her automatic denial. Now she remembered. "I saw the email and thought it was a scam."

"If it is, he's damn persistent. He tracked down Olive through a message board, then persuaded her to start the chain of connection. She brought him to me, and we ended up talking."

"About what?" Jessica tried to keep the suspicion out of her voice but didn't quite succeed.

"It's not like that," Greg said wearily. "Atherton didn't want to approach you directly since you hadn't responded to his messages. He wanted to talk to me to see if I thought it would be worth pursuing further or if it would only aggravate you."

"So, you told him that we weren't interested." It must have been a rough conversation. Someone persistent enough to follow through in person wouldn't have been dissuaded easily.

"Actually, I ended up listening to what he wanted to do. It doesn't sound like he's one of the same type of producers who screwed over your mom. He wants a facts-based program, one to educate people about real mediums and real ghosts."

"They all say they want facts but end up pushing sensationalism." Jessica's lip curled as if she could actually taste the bitterness on her tongue.

"Okay. If that's how you feel." Greg leaned forward and yawned. "I'm wiped. I ended up working two extra hours to make up the time I spent talking to Atherton. And it'll be an early start tomorrow. Bobby got fired today. I don't want to give Manuel an excuse to make me the next example."

"You look exhausted," she said quietly. "Guess it's my turn for a holiday." His roguish smile came and went too quickly to make much of an impact. "Maybe once the next couple of jobs are done."

He stripped off his dusty clothes and hit the shower. For once, his habit of walking around mostly naked didn't immediately inspire Jessica's libido. Instead, she felt guilty and uneasy. She and Greg had both been working a lot more than usual; it was wearing them both down. The pipes thumped to deliver a hot shower.

Knowing Greg would be occupied for a while, Jessica opened up her email and found the messages from Calvin Atherton.

From: catherton@paratv.org
To: info@gotghosts.com
Subject: Query re Spirit Sight

Ms. Miles, I was a big fan of your mother's show and I've been following your work for the last two years. You have an uncanny ability to explain the supernatural in terms that don't seem alarming or upsetting, and your clinical approach to ghost hunting is exactly what our network is looking for.

We would like to create a new version of Spirit Sight: Conversations from the Grave on our cable network and have you co-host the episodes. I will be in New York for the next few months and would be more than happy to meet with you to discuss the details.

The reply button hovered under her cursor, like a hungry maw ready to trap a buzzing insect. *We can't keep up this pace.* Jessica could never forget that every genuine haunting meant there was a real person, afraid and trapped between worlds. *Just because they're dead doesn't mean I can stop caring about them.* The families dealing with a haunting also had her sympathies, but they usually had plenty of living options to help them. The dead only had a few people who believed and even fewer with the skills and knowledge to provide aid.

"And then I can't say no," she said softly. The inquires poured into her mailbox, all desperately asking for help. Some were frauds or attention seekers, but there was no way to know which was which without doing an investigation.

But refusing to say no to the public meant saying no to herself and Greg. No to financial security. No to getting enough sleep to function. No to the freedom to focus on themselves rather than wearily trudging from job to job.

She stared at the closed bathroom door. Greg was a good judge of character. If he hadn't gotten an exploitative vibe from Calvin Atherton, then maybe the offer was legitimate rather than a smoke screen. *If I love him, shouldn't I be willing to listen, at the very least?* There was no doubt about the first part of the sentence. She loved Greg, and the guilt and concern over his health, both physical and mental, ate away at her moral high ground.

Taking a deep breath, she hit the reply button.

"I'm so glad you decided to meet with me, Ms. Miles. I was a great admirer of your mother's." Calvin Atherton was a compact man with deep set dark eyes and a contagious smile.

His shock of dark hair contrasted sharply with his pale skin. Reaching out, he took her hand in both of his. His skin was warm and dry, as if he'd been making bread without completely cleaning off the traces of flour.

"Thank you." Jessica glanced over at her manager. She wasn't due to start her shift at the Breakfast Bar for another hour, but it still seemed awkward sitting down when she was in uniform.

"And Mr. Cook! A pleasure to see you again." Calvin smiled and grasped Greg's hand in his double-handed shake.

Greg only nodded, his weariness still evident in his slumped posture. He could only stay for a little while. After yesterday's firing, testing Manuel's patience wasn't smart.

Jessica had tried to convince Calvin to meet with them later in the afternoon, but he'd insisted on doing it first thing. *Probably worried I'll change my mind if I give him time. Calvin looks like the executives I remember from my mother's show. Polished and with convincing but fake amiability.* With another glance at Greg, she reminded herself to keep an open mind.

"Let's get to business. Mr. Atherton. You admired my mother, which means you know what happened with her show. Why would I want to risk getting involved with another production?"

"Did Mr. Cook explain to you what I want

to do?" Calvin gestured at Greg, who was ignoring the food to focus on the man because he'd promised to follow Jessica's lead. If the producer said anything she didn't like, Greg would whisk her away at the slightest signal.

"Only in the broadest possible terms," she said. "You want to put my show on your cable network." Jessica didn't want to spend hours dancing around the subject. "I took a look at your lineup. Most of the shows you're broadcasting are horror stories with a slap-dash veneer of reality. You use dramatic recreations and emotionally charged interviews to make sure the audience checks in for every episode."

"I appreciate your bluntness and the homework you've obviously done." Calvin's cheerful smile hadn't slipped even a tiny bit. "Let me be equally blunt. People have been sharing scary ghost stories since we first sat around a fire. But those stories have changed over the years. These days, our audience has enough to be scared about in their real lives. Now they want to understand this new world of strange powers and even stranger occurrences. They want someone they can trust to tell them the truth, not someone who's going to see a spectral orb in every grain of dust. In short, they want you."

"And what happens if I demonstrate that there's no ghost in a particular investigation? Will you still air those episodes?" This was the key point. If they were only going to air the spectacular finds, then there would be pressure.

"Of course. That's where your co-host comes in. Have you heard of Keith Alban?" Calvin leaned forward, resting his elbows on the table.

The name rang a bell but not one easily placed. He wasn't one of the touring mediums or television psychics, or at least, not a successful one. Her brain dredged up a magazine article about tips to avoid falling prey to psychic scams. "He worked for the New Orleans police, in their division that goes after fake mediums."

"He did. Now he works for Special Investigations." Calvin beamed like a proud father.

Jessica grimaced. She'd had one encounter with Special Investigations, and one was more than enough for a lifetime. The agency regulated anything related to paranormal abilities and had a reputation for acting on fear. "If Special Investigations is involved—"

"They're not." Calvin hastened to assure her. "We approached Keith and he was the one who alerted us to your videos. He suggested pairing up with you."

"I certainly did." A young man approached their table, his easy grin suggesting he'd never been in a situation where he'd doubted his welcome. "It's nice to meet you, Jessica. And you must be Greg."

Greg squeezed her hand under the table, checking in to see if she wanted to call a halt to this meeting. She didn't like the sense of being ambushed, but she wasn't quite ready to walk away. *I owe both of us the chance at getting us out of this financial mess.*

She studied Keith as he ordered a drink from the server. He was handsome with long brown hair framing his face and a tall, lean frame, but he didn't seem to be particular self-conscious about it. *I wonder how powerful he is?* Her mother's gift had allowed her to regularly see and hear ghosts, but not reliably enough for her producers. Then there had been Bernie, the little girl that Jessica and Greg had helped to rescue before she could be snatched up by Special Investigations. The constant attentions of the dead had been mistaken for schizophrenia and while Bernie was a sweet girl, she also could be eccentric and prone to random outbursts. It seemed as if the more powerful a medium was, the more ghosts they attracted, and the more likely they would be overwhelmed.

Still, the more she watched Keith, the more she thought she could see the signs of something uncertain underneath his apparent confidence. The way he picked up the utensils far more quickly than necessary. Or how his smile seemed fixed in place, like he was afraid to drop it.

"People don't know what to think these days," he began, easily dominating the table. "Belief in all sorts of things is having a resurgence, from UFOs to Bigfoot to ghosts. The idea seems to be that if superpowers can be real, then what's to stop anything else from being real? Sadly, there are a lot of people trying to cash in on it."

"So I've seen." Jessica kept her face neutral. The Internet was full of people selling recordings, gadgets, and courses to enhance a person's latent psychic ability, or jury-rigged defenses against the so-called dangerous powers out there. All of them were about as reliable as products promising to help people lose weight without diet or exercise, or multi-level marketing schemes promising thousands of dollars in income.

"We want to help our audiences understand what could be happening to them. Almost forty percent of people believe they have personally had a paranormal encounter. Most of them are made to feel delusional or dismissed. We want to them to know they aren't alone." Calvin paused, tilting his head to one side. "I know you have a suspicious view of television after what happened to your mother. And I'll be the first to admit that there are a lot of exploitive shows out there. But that's not what we're looking to do."

Greg shifted in his seat. "Plans and results aren't always the same thing."

Keith didn't seem off-put by Greg's implicit challenge. "You're right. But good intentions are where things have to start."

Eager to avoid a testosterone-fueled posturing contest, Jessica brought the conversation back to the point. "So how do you think your show will be different?"

Calvin answered quickly. "To start with, we're going to approach each investigation from two angles. Keith will go in and use his abilities to sense any supernatural activity. Then we want you to go in from a scientific angle. Exactly the sort of thing that you've been doing already. Then the two of you will discuss the case on camera and explain the lore and science to our viewers."

"And we don't want a faith versus science debate either. The hope is that by using two different techniques, we'll both be less susceptible to hoaxes and wishful thinking," Keith added.

It's worked before. When she and Greg investigated the Rose on the Grave Bed and Breakfast, they'd captured what they thought was paranormal activity on camera, but the movement was caused by a telekinetic owner who believed she owned a building full of the ghosts of children who had been the victims of a tragedy.

217

This was a hard choice. Experience told her to run the other way and not look back. But the world had changed, and both Calvin and Keith seemed sincere in their desire to do the right thing. Maybe she needed to decide what was most important to her. If she continued to insist on complete control, she and Greg would keep plunging into debt. Or, she could take a chance on the opportunity to pursue her dreams and get paid to do so, but with the risk of seeing those dreams undermined, then sacrificed on the altar of entertainment.

She turned to Greg. He would support her no matter what she chose. That was reassuring, but it also placed the burden directly on her shoulders. Her decision would affect both of them long term.

"We can get through whatever we have to. Do what you need to do in order to sleep at night," he said quietly.

"All right." She turned back to Calvin and Keith. "I can do this, but I'll want some provisions written into the contract. If I'm involved, then the goal of the show needs to be education and helping people, not sensationalizing their pain or trying to make things seem more dramatic than they actually were."

Calvin grinned. "I'm so glad Keith insisted we come and talk to you directly. And I have no problem with your terms."

"We all want the same things." Keith's smile started to drop. "In fact, I think I might already have the perfect case for us to start with. Friends of my family, Phoebe and Herman Mulvey. They're an older couple whose daughter recently died, and now they're raising their grandson."

"What are they experiencing?" Jessica asked. "Everything seems to center around the baby. The crib will be moved in the middle of the night, even though Herman bolted it to the wall. They hear growling voices through the baby monitor, then Shawn starts to cry." Keith hesitated, his knuckles whitening around his fork. "I've been there and I'm sensing a dark presence. We could go there tonight to investigate."

"Tonight?" Jessica looked at Greg in surprise. *Nothing in television moves this fast.*

"It's a bit of a surprise, but there's no reason why not. I can run the cameras." Calvin's smile suddenly seemed a little strained around the edges. "Think of it like a trial run. If it doesn't work out, we'll pay you for your time. Two thousand dollars each for the night."

"Each?" Greg leaned forward. "And you'll get the same with every episode for the first season." Calvin beamed in deal-closing confidence.

"Please"—Keith bit his lip—"I know this is rushed, but the Mulveys have been like parents to me.

They're already struggling to cope with their daughter's death; now they're afraid for their grandson. You're exactly what they need."

The undercurrent of desperation in Keith's expression made Jessica want to run even though she couldn't walk away from someone who needed her help. But it didn't mean she was about to bolt carelessly into a bad situation. "Do you have the Mulvey's information here? We could meet you there after we're done work."

"Sure thing." Keith smiled in relief. He pulled a folded piece of paper out of his pocket and handed it over.

Jessica opened it and saw the Mulveys' names, address and most importantly, their home and cell numbers. She'd start the investigation a little early, without the cameras, to make sure that Calvin and Keith were what they said they were.

"Thank you for agreeing to see me." Jessica offered her hand to Phoebe Mulvey, who shook it firmly. The family was staying in a hotel. The necessity of it seemed to personally offend the doting grandmother.

"I'm glad you're here. I want whatever this thing is out of my house and away from my Shawnie." Phoebe Mulvey was a fierce grandmama bear who was not about to stand for some pesky ghost thinking it could frighten her grandson and get away with it. Jessica was surprised the woman hadn't driven out the ghost through her own sheer determined will.

"I don't blame you. He's adorable." Jessica smiled at baby Shawn, who gave her a milk-tooth-filled grin in return. "Why don't you tell me what happened?"

"At first, I thought I just wasn't used to having a baby in the house again," Phoebe said. "We used to babysit overnight sometimes for Louisa and Mark, but after the accident..."

Jessica hesitated, not wanting to poke at obviously fresh wounds, but the way a person died seemed to have a big impact on whether or not they became a ghost. "What kind of accident?"

"A car accident. Mark was driving, and the car hit the side of an overpass." Phoebe's mouth tightened. "Not to speak ill of the dead, but he had trouble with alcohol and drugs. Louisa tried to help him, but she had Shawn to think of."

A sudden, violent death was one of the more common ways to transition into a ghost. Some of the ghosts that her mother had spoken to hadn't even realized they were dead.

"Shawnie had always been such a good baby. He slept through the night when he was only two months old. When he was awake, he was just the sweetest thing." Phoebe planted a reflexive kiss on Shawn's head. "At first, I thought the accident had affected him because he would start to scream whenever we put him in the crib. I would have to rock him until he fell asleep, then sneak out of the room. A few minutes later, he'd wake up crying like his little heart was broken."

"Poor little guy."

"I thought he'd adjust, but it kept happening. He'd only sleep if I brought him into my room or if I stayed in his."

From there, the rest of the story matched what Keith had told them. Furniture moved, voices in the night. Jessica took notes and could understand Keith's concern. Spirits and babies could be a difficult combination. Most children saw the spirit world easily, making it easy for ghosts to frighten them. The ghosts then grew stronger from the child's fear and it could become a perpetuating cycle.

"Last night was the final straw." Phoebe's voice shook, and her arms circled little Shawn. "I've never backed down from a fight in my life, but I've never been so frightened."

"What happened?" *Keith and Calvin didn't mention anything in particular about last night.*

"Keith was there, trying to communicate with the ghost when the whole house began to shake. Shawn was with Herman, upstairs in the nursery, and both of them were screaming.

When Keith and I got upstairs, it was like a tornado inside the house. Shawn and Herman were in the middle, sitting in the rocking chair while blankets and diapers and such whirled around them." Irritation banished Phoebe's fear. "I started shouting, 'That's quite enough of that, thank you!' And it all stopped. Everything dropped to the floor."

Not surprising. Even though women were often encouraged to avoid conflict or self-assertion, older ladies such as Phoebe had reached the phase of their life where they were done with effacing themselves for society's expectations, and they became forces to be reckoned with.

"I got everyone out of the house and told Keith to find someone who could fix this." Phoebe sniffed. "That ghost absolutely ruined the wallpaper in Shawn's room. He ripped it to pieces."

"The ghost physically ripped the wallpaper off the wall?" Jessica wanted to make sure Phoebe wasn't exaggerating for effect.

Creating a wind to throw around light objects was one thing, but tearing up wallpaper would take more energy than most ghosts could manage.

"Big gouges all over the walls. It'll take a pretty penny to fix them." Phoebe frowned. "You said your young man worked in construction. Will he be repairing the walls?"

"I can talk to him," Jessica said cautiously, a little dazed by the rapid flow of assumptions. This didn't sound like a grieved parent who might be checking on Shawn from beyond the grave. Instead it was more reminiscent of the haunting at Greg's parents' home. "Mrs. Mulvey, do you collect antiques or go to estate sales?"

"I've worked hard all my life, and I'd much rather have something new made to my taste than something creaky and worn out. Even the house is new, built less than five years ago." Phoebe frowned, jiggling Shawn to keep him happy. "Why do you ask?"

"I'm trying to get a sense of where the ghost might have come from."

"I don't care where it came from. I want you to get rid of it." Phoebe stood up. "It's time for Shawn to eat. You'll be at the house tonight?"

"That's the plan," Jessica said cautiously.

"Good. Herman will meet you there. It's been a pleasure meeting you." Phoebe walked away before Jessica could do more than a half-hearted wave goodbye.

This is bigger than Keith and Calvin made us think. It wasn't a typical haunting anymore. It sounded much more like a poltergeist, but those tended to be linked to teenagers. *Or it could be another inhuman entity.*

Jessica wished she could talk to her mother. Inhuman entities were supposed to be incredibly rare. Most mediums never encountered them. Jessica had already dealt with one. *What are the odds of a second one?* Or maybe she was allowing herself to be spooked by her experiences.

Phoebe hadn't mentioned an oppressive atmosphere or electrical disturbances, and she didn't collect antiques or anything else connected with the occult. *Maybe it is a poltergeist. If Shawn's parents died violently, maybe their energy somehow translated into this kind of activity.* The uncertainty was the reason that investigations needed to be done.

"You!" a slurred male voice shouted. Jessica snapped out of her musings. A young man with blond hair and a stained t-shirt was stumbling toward her. He must have come out of the hotel bar. She quickly gathered her things. Someone who was already drunk by mid-afternoon wasn't a person she wanted to deal with.

"Sir," a man wearing a hotel name badge moved to intercept, but the drunk shoved past him.

"You're Cook's bitch." The drunk eyed her up and down. "Believes in ghosts and all that."

"Bobby?" Jessica said cautiously, guessing it was him from Greg's description. The hotel security guard was moving to stand between her and the drunk.

"Surprise." Bobby flashed her a sloppy vindictive smile. "Your asshole boyfriend got me fired."

"You did that yourself." She stepped back cautiously and faced the security guard. "I'd like to go now, please."

"Of course, miss. This way." He kept his body between her and Bobby, walking her swiftly to the lobby entrance.

"Don't you walk away from me! I'll make sure you're both sorry! I'll make sure the world knows…" Bobby's threats devolved into incoherent cursing and slurs. The onslaught might have been more effective if he hadn't tripped over his own feet and fallen flat on his face. But it was still enough to create a rigid band of uncertainty around Jessica's heart.

The security guard escorted her to a cab and made sure she was safe inside. "I'll take care of him, miss. You don't need to worry."

As the taxi pulled away, Jessica leaned back and exhaled. Between a prospective show, a violent ghost and the nasty drunk, this was turning into one heck of a day. She only hoped that it wasn't going to get worse.

"We should press charges." Greg wished he could have been there to protect Jessica. It would have been very satisfying to land a few self-defense punches on Bobby.

"I filed a report. If he does anything else, there will be a record." Jessica sighed as their truck pulled up in front of the Mulvey's home. "I'm okay. He didn't do more than scare me for a second."

The law might disagree, but Greg's inner caveman felt Bobby's actions were more than enough to justify punitive action. "It's not okay."

"He's a bully and a jerk who thrives on attention. Giving him any more only makes him happier. I don't want to waste time on it, not when we've got our hands full here." Jessica handed him a paper bag. "Salt. Just in case."

"Maybe we should see if we can find another priest who could do the exorcism rite." The bungalow seemed perfectly ordinary in the sunset glow, like any of the dozens of others on the street. The front windows were open and pale gauze curtains fluttered in the breeze. But every contractor knew how ordinary surfaces could conceal horrific rot or mold.

"There aren't that many. The Catholic Church doesn't even officially endorse them anymore. Father Thomas was one of a dying breed." Jessica winced. "Sorry. Bad phrase."

"At the first sign of trouble, we're out of there. Promise?" The idea of some evil spirit getting their hands on Jessica made Greg sick to his stomach.

"Promise," she said solemnly. "Though if Keith is a medium, he would have sensed it."

But would he have told us? Keith and Calvin had been eager to get them in and Greg didn't think it was because of prospective ratings. He followed Jessica up the flagstone walkway.

"Right on time." Calvin's hearty grin held a forced quality when he opened the door. Keith and an older man were waiting nearby.

"Mr. Mulvey, I'm sorry for your loss,"

Jessica said. "I'd like to see the nursery."

"It's down the hall here." Herman Mulvey pointed, his thick mustache bristling like salt-and-pepper wires. His head was mostly bare except for a gray fringe behind his ears, but he was still a powerful physical presence.

The room had probably been a cheerful place a few nights ago. The walls were covered with a wallpaper featuring happy clowns cavorting and dancing. The white crib, change table, and rocking chair could have come from a baby catalogue. But this nursery wasn't going to be featured in any magazines.

Something had ripped through the walls in long, deep parallel gashes, cutting through the wallpaper, plaster and going right into the drywall. The crib mattress was slashed, with wisps of batting clinging to the steel coils. The few toys in the room were broken and smashed. The circus-print curtains had been torn from the window and shredded.

"I was putting Shawn into the crib when the whole room started to shake like it was an earthquake," Herman said. "He woke up and I thought he was going to start screaming, but then it was like something frightened him too badly to make a sound."

Greg was starting to hate this ghost. Picking on children, ripping apart the room—they were the acts of a bully. Jessica always talked about having compassion for the dead, how frightening it must be to be cut off from everyone. But this spirit didn't deserve compassion. It deserved to be shoved into the light with both hands and the metaphysical door slammed behind it.

Movement to the side caught his attention. Calvin was slowly circling the group, a heavy camera raised to his eye. Like a vulture looking for a corpse. Greg lowered his gaze, feeling like a hypocrite. He'd convinced Jessica to give this show a chance, even though she'd explained her concerns about exploitation over and over. *What did I think would happen?* He and Jessica had agreed. The Mulveys had agreed.

"Everything was whirling around. I held Shawn and tried to find a way through where he wouldn't get hurt by the debris. That's when Phoebe made it stop," Herman finished.

"Greg, with your experience as a contractor, can you tell us about the marks in the wall? What would it take to make them?" Calvin asked.

The unblinking eye of the camera settled

on Greg. He walked over to the closest one and probed the slash with his fingers. It was nearly two feet long and felt deep enough to go into the studs. "It would take a lot of muscle and a sharp tool to do this much damage. If I tried to replicate it, I'd wear myself out pretty quickly. I wouldn't have been able to do all of these." He touched another long cut, this one shallower but much longer, nearly seven feet. "Someone would have had to run to make a cut like this one. It's all one long continuous slice."

"Phoebe mentioned hearing voices through the baby monitor. Did you hear any voices that night?" Jessica asked.

"Only the one on the tape." Herman gestured at Keith.

Keith flinched. Herman frowned in confusion.

"What tape?" Calvin asked in confusion.

Keith tried to wave it away. "It's nothing. Just an EVP session."

"An EVP?" To the casual observer, Jessica appeared reasonably calm. But Greg knew that particular note of diplomatic inquiry and recognized the signs of an imminent explosion.

"Not exactly," Keith turned beseeching eyes toward Calvin but there was no help from the producer.

"If you were investigating last night, why did you insist we come back tonight? And why didn't you turn over the footage?" Calvin pulled his head out from behind the camera, his eyes narrowing. "What's going on here?"

"If you recorded an EVP, then we need to hear it." Jessica's tone was one of syrup-coated steel. "Or Greg and I will be leaving right now."

Keith's shoulders dropped, and he pulled a digital recorder out of his pocket, his hand shaking as he pushed the play button.

There was a loud clatter, like footsteps leaving the room. Distant shouts punctuated the silence. Phoebe demanded to know what was going on. Then, all was still again.

A low rumble filled the air. Even through the miniscule speakers on the recorder, it seemed to vibrate with bass. An animalistic growl spoke, "Tell Jessica and Greg that I'm looking forward to playing with them again." Inhuman laughter followed until Keith shut off the recording.

Greg knew that voice. He'd had nightmares about that voice. "It's not possible."

"That's not electronic voice phenomena." Jessica's hand slipped into his, squeezing it hard to remind him that he wasn't alone.

"You said they knew. That you'd worked with them, and they'd be able to help us."

Herman's flat tone was more accusatory than yelling would have been.

"I did. I lied. I lied to you and to Calvin." Keith wearily turned to face Jessica. "I didn't think you'd come if you knew what was waiting here."

So, he let us walk into a dangerous situation unprepared. Greg shook with anger. "What the hell is wrong with you?"

"I—"

Calvin cut Keith off. "This isn't how we do business. I'm sorry."

"I didn't want to frighten you away." Keith raised a pleading gaze in her direction.

"Everything I could sense told me that we needed your help with this, that you two were the only people with a chance against whatever is in this house."

"You had no right to keep this from us," Jessica hissed. "We're leaving."

Greg's feet were strangely reluctant to shift from their places on the warped floor. It was as if he'd grown roots fastening him in place.

"We should stay."

Jessica's mouth opened in surprise. "What?"

"If the voice on the recording is what we think it is"—it was easier not to say the words *demon box* aloud—"then it will come after us no matter what."

"It can't be the same entity. We sealed it up and Father Thomas buried it. Unless…" Jessica fumbled for her phone with stiff fingers, setting the speaker so they all could hear.

Luckily Ellie answered on the first ring.

"Hi Jessica, I'm afraid we haven't finalized the funeral arrangements—"

"When Father Thomas died, was he in the graveyard?" Jessica interrupted.

"Yes. Near the big rowan tree."

Greg's throat dried. Jessica closed her eyes to ask the next question. "Did the police find anything else?"

"Plenty of damage. They knocked over headstones and smashed the grave offerings."

"Was there a box? A wooden box, wrapped in duct tape?" Greg demanded.

"Why, yes! It's so odd what some people will leave on graves. I don't know what they could have been thinking. The duct tape ruined the finish." Ellie clucked in aesthetic disapproval.

Greg fought the urge to vomit. *If she can bring us the box, then we have a chance.*

"A shame the whole thing was smashed to pieces." Ellie's words slew their final hopes. "I threw it—"

The call abruptly terminated with the dull beep of a dying battery.

"I'm so sorry," Keith whispered. "Could it have caused Father Thomas to have a heart attack?" Greg asked, the hollowness in his chest making it difficult to breathe.

"The timing still doesn't work. The Mulveys have had problems for months." Jessica insisted stubbornly, reaching up to cup Greg's face with both of her hands. "We don't have to stay here right now. We can go and come back

233

with the tools we need."

The last two words were directed at Keith, who had the grace to blush and stare at his shoes in embarrassment.

"What about us?" Herman asked.

"Mr. Mulvey, I don't know what's happening here, but it's much more dangerous than we expected. We need to leave while we still can." Jessica tugged at Greg's arm.

"You're right." The roots holding his feet crumbled. "Come on!"

All five of them ran down the hall toward the front door. Greg pulled it open, ready to herd everyone outside. But the handle jerked out of his hand, and the door slammed closed.

The open windows slid shut with clicks like the closing of a coffin lid.

"Too late!" a harsh growl echoed. The walls started to creak. Pictures shook and fell. The furniture began to rattle, scraping against the floor. The large ornamental mirror in the front hall crashed to the ground, shattering into thousands of pieces. More glass crashed in other rooms. *It's getting rid of the mirrors, so we can't trap it again.*

"Hello, Jessica and Greg. So good to see you again." The voice seemed to be coming from everywhere at once.

Icy fear gripped Greg, trying to freeze him in place. He muscled through the paralysis,

moving to stand in front of Jessica. He

wasn't going to let this creature get her. *I threw myself on the grenade once before. I'll do it again if I have to.*

"Who are you?" Keith demanded.

"Names aren't important." It laughed.

Names bind it. Greg might still be an apprentice when it came to ghosts, but he remembered that bit of trivia.

"This is my house and whatever you are, you aren't welcome here," Herman Mulvey thundered. "Get out!"

For a moment, the creaking and rattling stopped and there was silence. Greg didn't dare to hope the situation would be that simple.

The answer, when it came, reverberated through their feet. "No."

Faced with her worst nightmare, Jessica found herself surprisingly calm and alert, her mind dispassionately and swiftly sorting through possibilities. The entity was powerful, angry and unpredictable. If they couldn't leave the house, they needed a sanctuary. "Everyone, go to the kitchen."

Herman scowled at her. "Wh—"

"She's right." Keith grabbed the older man's arm and got him moving.

The entity cackled. "You can't hide from

me."

"We're not hiding," she said grimly, walking backward slowly. Bits of glass crunched under her shoes. Calvin had already hurried after Herman and Keith. Greg was behind her, his hand resting on her shoulder blades to guide her around furniture or any threat.

Once they stepped onto the cream-colored linoleum, Jessica's attention snapped to Herman. "Where's the salt?"

"Under the cupboard." He pointed, obviously confused.

"I've got it." Greg grabbed the plain white cylinder. Jessica took the bag of salt out of her pocket and poured it carefully across the threshold. The entity howled and the inanimate objects in the household started their unearthly cacophony again.

Beside her, Greg poured out more salt, creating a line along the walls. Keith grabbed the salt cellar from the kitchen table and started sealing the other side. Thankfully, the kitchen was small enough to finish quickly.

"What does the salt do?" Calvin asked, aiming the camera in her direction.

"Ghosts can't cross a salt threshold. We don't know why, but it's been used to create protective spaces for thousands of years," she explained. The light overhead began to blink on and off. "It will be able to control the electrical system, but it shouldn't be able to come in here."

"Shouldn't?" Herman didn't sound impressed.

"When it comes to ghosts, so much of our understanding is mixed up in mythology and what makes a good story. There aren't many people who have tried to separate fact from fiction." Jessica took a deep breath. "We've bought ourselves some time to figure out what to do next."

"My cell phone is dead. The battery's been drained." Greg shoved the useless rectangle back in his pocket. Jessica checked hers and discovered it was similarly drained. *It drained the phones but not the camera?* Something tickled at the edge of her awareness.

"It wasn't here before last night, I swear it." Keith shoved his hair out of his face with impatient fingers. "There was something, but it wasn't anything like the darkness I feel now."

"Two spirits?" Greg glanced at her for confirmation. "We've seen that before."

"Maybe." Jessica sat down at the kitchen table and pointed at Keith and Calvin. "You need to tell me exactly what happened the other night with the EVP session."

She tried not to let her lip curl in disgust when Keith sat down. Calvin stayed upright to continue filming. Keith folded his hands on the table. "I'd done a cleansing for Herman and Phoebe, but it didn't have any effect. I thought maybe the ghost needed to communicate something before it could move on. So, I tried one session that night, but I didn't get anything. I called Calvin to see if he'd had any luck getting through to you."

"Then what happened?" she asked.

"He said he hadn't. I hung up, the lights started to flicker and then I could sense a much stronger presence than before. I tried a second EVP session, and you heard what happened." Keith shook his head. "What are you thinking?"

"There must be a reason it came here. When it was haunting Greg's parents' home, it was because his father had bought a demon box at an estate sale. He thought it was a colorful description. It wasn't. When he opened it, the entity inside escaped, but it couldn't leave the house. So why is it here? It was buried in St. Michael's cemetery."

"That's where Shawn was baptized. It's only a few hundred yards through the woods out back," Herman said.

"Okay. I can see a working hypothesis that when the entity broke free, it started looking for us. If Keith and Herman were talking about us, our names could have drawn it to this house. Or maybe it was just because it was close." There were a lot of holes, but until a better idea presented itself, she'd stick with it. "Either way, it doesn't matter. It's here now."

"I think the bigger question is, how can we

stop it?" Greg asked. "It broke all the mirrors, and we don't have another demon box to hold it in."

"If we can contain it, we'd have a chance to bring in outside help and supplies." Jessica winced as more glass broke elsewhere in the house.

"What does it want?" Calvin asked.

Jessica remembered the slimy feel of the creature in her mind when it had possessed her body. Its mind had been disjointed, scattered, driven by emotional reaction.

"It wants attention. And power," Greg said slowly. "It could be why it hasn't hurt us. It craves an audience."

Which is why it left the camera functioning. And it was also a logical assumption for why it hadn't attacked them directly. It could clearly tear apart walls, so human flesh shouldn't be a challenge. Most paranormal experts believed ghosts rarely physically attacked beyond a few minor bruises and scratches. *Though how would we know if one had launched a fatal attack? There could be unsolved murders where ghosts are the murderers We'd never know for sure.*

"We can't assume we're safe. It might have killed Father Thomas," Greg said hesitantly.

"He died of a heart attack. That's not the same. He'd had heart trouble before and a bypass last year." It was so frustrating not knowing what the real possibilities were. Jessica ground her teeth.

"But if we're in here, it can't get us?"

Herman's voice was shaky.

Mom always said that belief and the will behind an action was as important as the action or tool. They need to believe. Even if she wasn't entirely certain. "Yes. We're safe."

"For now," the entity growled from the hall. "It can't cross the salt line," she said more confidently. *If it could, it would. It's got no reason to hold back.*

As the minutes ticked by with no immediate evidence she was wrong, Jessica breathed a sigh of relief. They could still hear sounds of destruction coming from the rest of the house, yet nothing crossed the threshold into the kitchen.

But we can't stay in the kitchen forever. "We need to figure out what we know."

Calvin immediately swung the camera toward her. "Do you really think this is the time to record?" she snapped. "Not really a moment of compelling television."

Calvin didn't lower the camera; however, he did shift his focus from the viewfinder to her face. "I wanted to do this show in order to educate people about what's out there. There are all kinds of amateur paranormal investigators, and some of them are finding more than they can handle. I want to let people know that ghosts aren't entertainment—they can be dangerous. When they see this footage, they'll know what real ghosts are like."

Does education actually require footage with a spooky voiceover? She wanted to yell at him. The words were on the tip of her tongue, ready to fly like poisoned daggers. It would be easy to dredge up accusations of exploitation, of profiting on the pain of others, of pushing the boundaries to get ratings. It was all there, all the frustration and anger that had been slowly boiling up for over twenty years, just waiting for a victim.

Except I'm not that kind of person. The voice of caution inside her head struggled to be heard amid the whirling emotional chaos.

"This is my fault." Keith's voice was ragged with guilt. "I felt it, but I didn't say anything. Instead I pushed Calvin to bring you in when all the time I knew there was something in this house waiting for its turn, for the light to fade and the rules to change."

His words didn't sound like the confident medium they'd spoken to earlier today. Jessica fought to think clearly through her anger. Her eyes sought Greg. He stood beside the counter, the muscles in his neck and arms so rigid, they seemed like they could burst. Shiny sweat gleamed on his forehead and cheeks, and his gaze was constantly darting around the room.

He's terrified. Keith is guilty. Calvin's consumed with ambition. Herman's lips were locked between his teeth as his hands shook violently. *He's trying to hold something back. And I'm furious enough to punch through the wall.*

"It's amplifying our emotions." She spoke the words aloud. "It's trying to drive us into a state where we're not thinking, just reacting."

"How can we fight something like that?" Keith's teary eyes lifted to meet hers.

A snarled insult nearly flew from Jessica's lips, but she caught herself in time. "We have to make sure we stay aware of it. And we need to focus on facts and logic instead of how we feel."

"Can a ghost get into our heads?" Herman asked. "The truth is, we don't know what ghosts can and can't do." Jessica wasn't sure if the sudden swamping of despair was the entity's influence or the result of her genuine helplessness. She missed the vigor of her anger. "There's so much myth and outright fraud that it's a full-time job just to separate genuine hauntings from wishful thinking or hoaxes."

Herman jumped up from the table. "So, you don't know anything for sure?"

"I know some things but not as much as I'd like." She took a deep breath. "Not every death creates a ghost. It seems to be more likely if a death is sudden or violent."

"Ghosts don't seem to last for a long time. Most hauntings are less than a hundred years old," Keith added. "There are a few older ones, but they mostly seem to be residual hauntings rather than active spirits."

"You said that there's a theory about inhuman entities, how they could be spirits who have forgotten they were once human." Greg straightened. "What if we can remind this one of who he used to be? Could he go into the light then?"

"I'm not sure it'll let us out to do the research." Her words came out sharper than she'd intended, so she tried to soften them. "But it's a good idea."

"Ghosts can't cross a salt barrier. Or certain mystical symbols." Keith tapped his fingers on the table.

"Stone seals them in." A smile flickered around her mouth. "And duct tape."

Greg smiled at her, easing some of the sense of crushing horror.

Herman stood up to open one of the cupboards. "Stone traps them, you said?"

"Yes." Jessica glanced at the others. "Do you think this would work?" Herman pulled out a heavy marble bowl, setting it gently on the counter.

There's no lid. And even if there were, they didn't have anything to bind it with.

A loud crash from the back of the house made them all jump.

"That sounded different." Keith's long fingers curled over the bowl's edge, ready to hurl it at the entity if it might help.

A man's hoarse scream ripped through the house.

Greg didn't pause to think. If he had, he knew the paralyzing terror from before would have locked him in place. He jumped over the line of salt on the threshold, running toward the ruined nursery.

Jessica shouted behind him, but the words were indistinct and distant. The house didn't have the same aura from their earlier retreat to the kitchen. The air was somehow emptier but also more menacing, like they'd traded one danger for something even deadlier.

He skidded to a stop outside the nursery. A man was sprawled on the ground, his limbs twisted in a way that didn't seem physically possible. He was screaming and writhing in incredible torment.

"Hey! Leave him alone!" Not exactly a formal exorcism. Hopefully the intent would be enough.

The man flipped over, and Greg stumbled back at the sight of a pale leprous face with dark sunken eyes. The fear he'd been suppressing rose up and locked icy hands around his throat.

Warmer hands grabbed at him from behind.

"Greg! We have to get back to the kitchen."

The man curled into a ball and the screams faded to whimpers.

Something didn't seem right. Greg took a closer look at the man. The skin on his face was mottled white, but his hands were a healthy tan. "It's makeup."

"What?" Jessica pushed past him, bending down to examine their uninvited guest. "You're right. It's stage makeup."

The man's eyes opened, and he cackled. Greg snatched Jessica with both hands, moving her to the relatively safety behind him.

Moving stiffly, like a puppet with an unskilled puppeteer, the man got to his feet. He held up his hands in front of him, flexing the fingers. Footsteps pounded down the hall and Herman, Keith, and Calvin appeared. Calvin still held the camera to his eye and the steady red light meant it was all being recorded.

As the man stepped forward, Greg finally saw the shape of the face beneath the makeup. A familiar face. "Bobby?"

"Not anymore." It was Bobby's voice but far harsher and crueler. This wasn't a petty bully speaking. It was something evil. "He was planning to frighten you and make you look like fools. A pathetic plan for a pathetic waste of a man. But I can think of far more interesting things to do with this flesh."

It sounded like the sort of thing Bobby

would come up with. Meaningless one-upmanship to bolster his own ego by shoving someone else down. Greg allowed himself a fleeting moment of regret. Even a jerk didn't deserve a fate like this. "You're not going anywhere."

Bobby's mouth widened in a smile that seemed to hold far too many teeth. "My dear boy... you can't stop me any longer."

"Oh my God," Keith whispered.

"Having a body doesn't mean you can get past us," Jessica challenged the entity, her eyes flashing with fury. "You're not going to be able to do any of your tricks anymore."

"I might not. But he can." The entity used Bobby's finger to point behind them.

Frigid air crawled along the floor, snaking around their legs. The studs inside the walls began to creak as they twisted and warped. Greg didn't want to take his eyes off the thing in Bobby's body, but he turned to see what was coming down the dark hallway.

It was another man. This one was insubstantial, flickering from one position to the next. His dark hair was slicked back to his skull, and rough stubble darkened his cheeks and chin. He laughed, but the eerie sound was disconnected from the movements of his mouth, like they were watching a badly dubbed movie.

"Mark?" Herman's fists clenched.

"Hey there, Dad." Mark laughed again. "You always hated when I called you that."

Greg's heart was pounding so hard that the roar threatened to drown out everything else. *How can I get Jessica out safely?* The entity wanted to hurt both of them. The first time it had been unleashed, it had threatened to torture each of them in order to hurt the other.

"Mark has been here for quite a while. He invited me to join him," the entity said.

"You promised you would help me kill them and get my son," Mark hissed.

"And I will. You can take one of them and have your vengeance."

"You're not getting Shawnie." Herman glared at the ghost. "I always tried to respect you for Louisa and Shawn's sakes, but you were a piss-poor excuse for a husband and father. You didn't deserve either of them."

Jessica squeezed Greg's hand and whispered. "Can you distract them?"

"You always did have a stupid way of seeing the world." Mark laughed. "It was your fault that Louisa got all these uppity ideas. Like I was supposed to be happy to be changing diapers and driving a minivan."

"It's what fathers are supposed to do." Greg stepped forward, shifting his shoulders to block the entity's view of the hall. Jessica's hand slipped out of his.

"Louisa thought so, too." Mark smirked.

"Always the nagging bitch."

"Stop talking about my daughter." Herman stepped in front of Mark's face. The ghost vanished.

Only to appear behind him. "She promised to stay with me until death do us part. I reminded her of that."

"What did you do?" Calvin asked from behind the camera.

"She was going to leave him," Herman said. His chin was high with pride despite the tears trickling down his cheeks.

"She thought I didn't know. I always knew all of her secrets." Mark vanished again.

"He killed her." The entity smiled, pulling Bobby's lips far too thin.

"Why come back then?" Keith demanded.

Greg resisted the urge to check and see where Jessica was. *Hopefully she's got a plan.*

Because he had no idea how they were supposed to contain the situation.

"Unfinished business." Mark's disembodied voice floated down the hall. "The brat was supposed to be with us, but I got impatient. He's mine, just like Louisa was."

"Neither of them is yours. They never were," Herman shouted.

Mark reappeared in front of the old man and plunged his insubstantial hand into Herman's chest. He grinned as Herman gasped and went pale.

"No!" Greg shouted, grabbing Herman and yanking him out of the ghost's reach. The old man collapsed, wheezing heavily. His gnarled hands painfully twisted the skin on Greg's arms, but Greg hung on grimly until Herman regained his feet.

Something hard jabbed him from behind. Greg spun to put himself between Herman and whatever approached.

Bobby's head twisted at an angle that seemed dangerously close to snapping his human neck. "Always the protector, Greg. Even when it would be far smarter to stay out of it."

He planted his hands on Greg's chest. Greg braced himself but wasn't worried. Bobby was a lot smaller physically.

The shove sent him flying backward down the hall. Greg's head hit the floor and pinpricks of light swam in front of his eyes.

"Did you think I was limited by this body?" The thing in Bobby laughed in cruel delight. "This host is eager to see what I can do to you. He has some interesting suggestions."

"Doesn't he care about you damaging his body?" Keith shouted. "You could end up injuring him permanently."

Bobby's body halted in mid-step, his face twisting. Greg hoped the pause meant that Bobby was trying to re-exert control.

"I don't have that problem." Mark suddenly appeared in front of Greg. "Your body seems like a good one."

"Ask your buddy." Greg rolled into a crouch, trying not to wince at the new bruises. "He thought so, too, and it didn't work out for him. I'm like one of those fast-flip houses. It might seem like a bargain, but it's more trouble than it's worth."

"Louisa felt sorry for you." Keith's words stopped Mark's ghostly fingers before they could plunge into Greg's chest.

Mark vanished and reappeared in front of Keith. The ghost looked more insubstantial than it had before, the edges wisping and roiling like smoke.

"She wanted to help you since you weren't strong enough to stay away from drugs and booze. She told me." Keith glared at the translucent Mark.

"They're trying to distract us," the entity spat.

"And who do you think is going to save you?" Mark sneered.

"Me, for one," Jessica's voice rang out through the house.

The relief that swept through Greg was nearly enough to knock him off his feet. Jessica stood in the hallway, braced and ready for battle. She held a wooden box in her hands, one of the cheap ones that people could pick up at craft stores and decorate themselves. Pale blue paint picked out the imprint of a baby's hand on the lid, along with the words, "My Precious Shawn."

"You can't possibly be expecting a piece of junk like that to work?" The entity laughed. "It took them months to craft the first box, imbuing layers and layers of power into the wood and ensuring there were no cracks to escape through."

"Desperate times call for desperate measures." Jessica slowly raised the lid. "A determined will is the most important tool when dealing with spirits."

"Except I'm not only a spirit. I have a body now, and it's quite comfortable." The entity flexed Bobby's fingers. "It will take more than your will to contain me."

Greg tensed, preparing to launch himself. If that thing took one step toward Jessica, then it was going through the wall. He didn't care if it attacked him or even if it killed him as long as she was safe.

"I know." Jessica pulled a tiny gold cross on a chain out of the box. "That's why I'm calling on reinforcements."

The sullen, dangerous atmosphere filling the house suddenly seemed to dissipate, like a fresh wind sweeping aside a curtain. Mark flickered in place, his snarling expression shifting to one of uncertainty. Bobby seemed smaller and frailer, backing away one staggering step at a time.

Keith grabbed the possessed man and held

him in place as he stared at an empty stretch of floor. "It's good to see you again."

Every hair on Greg's body tried to stand up in unison and his skin was pebbled with goosebumps. Something was here, even if he couldn't see it. He abruptly became aware of Calvin, still crouched at the end of the hall and capturing everything on camera. Jessica's hand on Greg's arm distracted him.

"Are you okay?" she asked. "I'm fine. What's happening?" He checked on Mark, who seemed to be contained and shrieking soundlessly.

"I took a chance that maybe a ghost would be able to fight another ghost." Jessica held up the cross. "I noticed this in Herman and Phoebe's bedroom and realized Father Thomas would have baptized Shawn if the ceremony was at St. Michael's. I used the cross as a talisman to summon him."

"Shawn?" Herman frowned.

"Father Thomas," she explained.

"Except Father Thomas didn't become a ghost, did he?" Greg wasn't going to complain if it was working, but he wanted to know if it would continue to keep the spirits at bay.

"No," Keith answered, shaking his head as he struggled to explain. "He's not lingering. It's more like he came back to quickly pick up something he left behind."

As Keith spoke, Mark suddenly vanished

and didn't reappear.

"No!" the entity shouted. "One down." Keith turned grimly to face the possessed man.

"You can't make me leave!" It bared Bobby's teeth. "He surrendered willingly!"

Greg sensed something powerful in the air around his former coworker, surrounding and containing him.

Jessica's hand crept into his. "I can almost make it out. It's like trying to see something behind a swaying bead curtain. There are only tiny pieces that I can make out at any one time, but I'm getting a sense of what lies beyond what I can see."

"Father Thomas says that Mark won't be bothering Shawn anymore," Keith reported. "He's been delivered to the light and taken for judgment."

"And what about the thing inside Bobby? Can he get rid of it?" Greg asked.

"He's trying." Keith said.

"What happens if we can't separate them?" Calvin asked from behind the camera.

Jessica rubbed at her cheek. "Bobby's soul will eventually be smothered by the spirit possessing him."

Greg wasn't feeling particularly charitable. His knee-jerk reaction was that Bobby had made his bed, and the asshole could burn in it. He'd threatened Jessica, made Greg's life miserable, and had been a generally shitty excuse for a human being. It was on the tip of Greg's tongue to say they should walk away. Until he remembered the slimy feel of the entity in his own head. He turned to face the possessed man. "Bobby, I know you can hear me."

The body jerked in reaction, hissing.

"Bobby's not here."

Greg stared into angry, demented eyes. There was no trace of the man he'd known, but when the entity had possessed him, Greg had been able to see and hear everything happening around him. He couldn't fight the spirit for more than a second or two at a time, yet he'd always been aware of every excruciating detail. "Yes, he is. Bobby, I don't know what you were planning to do here, but this can't be what you wanted."

"You think so?" the entity taunted. "He hates you. He wants to see everything you care about destroyed. He wants you broken."

"But neither of you can hurt us." Jessica moved to stand beside Greg, sliding her hand into his. Her steadfast certainty helped to anchor him. "The only way for Bobby to win is to push you out."

"If he tries, I'll scar this mind and leave him drowning in his own spit." The entity's mouth twisted in another inhuman grin. "You'll never be rid of me. I walked this earth for millennia before I was imprisoned. No matter how long

254

you wait, it will only be an eyeblink for me."

"And what happens to you if you scar his mind?" Herman stomped forward. "You'd be stuck in there, wouldn't you? I've seen people in vegetative states. They can live for decades with modern medicine."

For the first time, the entity hesitated. "You're lying."

"Bobby knows we're not," Keith said. "The tighter you hold on to this body, the more likely you are to damage it. None of us think you'll go quietly. Once the body dies, you'll come after us again. So, we'll make sure he keeps on breathing, no matter how many machines we have to hook him up to."

"Bobby, after working with you for six months, I can confidently say that you are one of the most stubborn, mule-headed bastards I have ever met." Greg hoped it wasn't too late. "Are you going to let this whiny ghost beat you?"

"No." The word came out of Bobby's mouth, and his limbs began to flail wildly.

"Fight it, Bobby! Drive it out!" Jessica shouted.

Neither Bobby nor the demon seemed to have enough control to speak. Grunts and shrieks filled the air as the body writhed on the floor.

Keith held out his hand. "Give me the cross!"

Jessica handed it over and Keith dropped to the floor and began to hesitantly recite in Latin, pressing the cross into Bobby's forehead.

Father Thomas's ghost must be telling him what to say. Greg bent, putting his knees and weight onto Bobby's shoulders. He grabbed the man's wrists and pinned them into place. Jessica immediately caught one of the legs in mid-kick and sat on it. Herman dropped onto the other.

The three of them managed to hold the body down while Keith chanted.

Greg added his own encouragement. "Come on, Bobby. Are you going to give this thing the satisfaction of beating you? You and I never got along, but this is your chance to do the right thing. Kick that ghost to the curb. You can do it."

Foam flecked Bobby's lips with each scream. He shook, trying to knock them off balance and get free.

Keith finished chanting in a triumphant crescendo. They all held their breaths.

The body shuddered and went limp. Greg fought the urge to snatch away his hands. Touching Bobby's skin was like handling something coated with old, grimy grease. The horrible slickness felt as if it was tainting Greg's own skin in a way that could never be scrubbed clean.

"Oh my God." Jessica retched but hung on grimly. Keith's hand clapped over his mouth and his shoulders heaved.

"What is it?" Greg demanded.

"Be grateful you can't see it." Jessica shook her head. "I can only glimpse the edges and it's... I might never eat anything ever again. It's evil."

Since Greg felt like he'd plunged his hands into the most disgusting, putrefying substance ever created, he could agree whole-heartedly with the sentiment. Every instinct screamed to let go and run away, but he made himself hang on. I won't let this thing loose to hurt anyone else. No matter what.

"Father Thomas says to keep holding him." Keith managed to repeat the message through clenched teeth.

Warmth stole over Greg's back, as if he was kneeling in the spring sun. Golden light filled the hallway.

Jerking his head up, Greg stared at the darkened windows in confusion. It was still night, and the Mulveys had blue-white lights in their fixtures. There shouldn't be anything in the hall that would cast a soft, yellowish glow. Yet, as impossible as it seemed, Bobby's body seemed to lay in sunshine.

For a second, Greg could have sworn he heard someone chuckle under his breath. Then the greasy, repugnant sensation began to vanish. In a few seconds, there was only cool skin and crackly arm hair under Greg's hands.

"You can let go," Jessica said softly, staring at the ceiling with tears shining in her eyes. "They took him."

Keith was staring upward with an equally rapt expression. "I've never seen anything like it."

"What about him?" Herman demanded. Greg looked down at Bobby's slack face and quickly pressed his fingers against the man's neck. To his relief, he found a weak but steady pulse. "He's still alive."

"He did it in the end. He pushed the spirit out." Keith scrubbed at his face with both hands. "Between him and Father Thomas, we got it out. And then, they took him."

"Who? Father Thomas?" Greg asked, not understanding.

"Not just him. There was something else with him." Jessica slowly got to her feet. "I guess I shouldn't be surprised. If there are demons, why can't there be angels?"

"And that's why it's important to check for copper piping or faulty insulation on your wiring before using an EMF reader." Jessica smiled gently at the camera. "If you're consistently getting high readings in one particular area, then make sure to search for an explanation besides a ghost."

"And we're clear." Miles, the camera operator, stepped away from the unit. "Good take."

"Thanks." Jessica moved away from the table where she'd been demonstrating how an EMF reader could be affected by non-otherworldly electrical fields. It still seemed wrong to leave everything without at least attempting to tidy up, even after a dozen different explanations of the union regulations surrounding filming. *At least it means that other people have work.* "Do we need to do any other spots?"

"Nope. That was the last one. I'll see you next week." Miles grinned at her before signaling to his crew to come and prepare the set for Keith's spots.

It's certainly different than when Mom did her show. Jessica lingered, feeling nostalgic. But she wouldn't trade her closed set for a studio audience, no matter how much the network hinted about improved ratings. It might have been exciting to watch people line up for the chance to be in the same room as her mother, but without the pressures to perform, Jessica was able to keep *Spirit Sight* moving in a more educational direction.

After the nightmare of the Mulvey's and the entity from the demon box, she'd fully expected Calvin to disappear along with his offer of television fame. Scripted sensationalism was one thing. Real life and death confrontations with a malevolent spirit was something else. Bobby had never regained consciousness after the possession and was in a hospital on life support.

Jessica still wasn't sure how she felt about him. It was hard to feel sorry when he'd been such a consistent jerk, and the only memory she had of him before the possession was when he'd decided to confront her in the hotel. But at the same time, he'd managed to do at least one noble act and helped them to destroy the entity. *Figuring out if one grand gesture makes up for a lifetime of asshole is above my paygrade.* She was happy to leave the entire mess in higher hands and focus on her new life.

Working in front of the cameras had come more naturally than she could have imagined. And she genuinely liked the messages she got from viewers and fans. Calvin handled all of the network pressure and negative aspects of the show. He'd become a fervent advocate about needing to educate the public about ghosts and what to do when someone suspected a haunting. He'd confronted the network and gotten them to pull some of their more exploitive shows and give *Spirit Sight* a prime timeslot and promotion. He'd taken the footage from the Mulvey home and after twenty minutes of viewing, the executives had agreed to his every demand. When the ratings for *Spirit Sight* started coming in, the executives were even more eager to please. It had become a viral phenomenon.

Calvin was right. People wanted to know what was out there. She was making enough money to quit her job at the diner, and Greg was back to

having the freedom to walk away from a job if the pain in the ass factor got too large. They were saving for a house, something with a little more room than the one-bedroom apartment.

"Hey. I thought you'd be out the door once they said, 'Cut.'" Keith grinned at her. Wardrobe had dressed him in a very scholarly tweed jacket and button-down shirt. "Are we still grabbing dinner before we do the investigation at the Lee house tonight?"

"Absolutely. I'm starving." Getting enough sleep had jump-started her appetite these days. She spotted Greg coming into the studio, making his way toward them. "Have you heard from the Mulveys?"

"Phoebe sent an email with a picture of Shawn. He's starting to talk." Keith bit his lip, glancing around. "Oh, Greg. I'm glad you're here."

This isn't like Keith. Why is he so nervous? Maybe the network had been putting pressure on him.

Greg crossed the final few yards, coming up behind Keith. "Is everything okay?"

"It's all fine." Keith hesitated. "I have a message and I thought you'd want to hear it together."

"From the network?" Jessica frowned. "I've told them I think the studio audience is a bad idea—"

"Not the network." Keith shook his head. "From your mom."

Jessica went still. Greg's hands crept around her shoulders and his warmth steadied her.

"Ever since what happened at the Mulvey's house, I've changed," Keith explained. "It's like I've been retuned, and now I don't just see and hear ghosts who are trapped on the mortal plane. I also get messages from ghosts who have gone into the light. Not all the time, but it keeps happening. And, well, last night, I got one that I think is from your mom."

"What did she say?" Jessica tried not to wonder if her mother was disappointed. They hadn't parted on the best terms.

"She said she's proud of you and happy for you both." Keith smiled, and the teasing light returned to his eyes. "She also says she would have been a kick-ass grandmother."

"Ha, ha. Very funny." Greg rolled his eyes. "See you tonight at dinner."

Keith left to begin shooting his individual segments for the show.

"I never did think that we'd get baby pressure from the dead parents. At least mine are more than happy to stay grandbaby free for the immediate future," Greg mock-grumbled,

262

until he noticed that Jessica still hadn't moved. "Are you okay?"

"Yeah." She made herself exhale. *Don't get too excited.* Messages from the dead were not medically reliable, and she'd only begun to suspect this morning.

"Are you sure?" Greg asked, smoothing her hair back from her face before snugging his hands on her hips. "You're all pale. If he upset you—"

"It's not that. It does sound like something my mom would have said." She took a deep breath. "But maybe we should stop at the drug store before we go to dinner."

"Why?" he asked in the adorable clueless way that made her want to hug him and shake her head in frustration at the same time.

She stared up, waiting for the mental gears to click into place.

His hands tightened on her hips, pulling her blouse taut across her belly.

There it is. She smiled at the man who'd won her heart somewhere between their one-night stand and calling her a fraud. He was everything she had needed without knowing it. *A true partner, ready to support me no matter what.* She loved him more than she could have imagined was possible.

"Are you kidding?" His expression was caught somewhere between hopeful and terrified.

"Well, I'm not sure." She shrugged one shoulder, still smiling at him. "That's why I think we should pick up a pregnancy test rather than relying on my dead mother's opinion."

He picked her up, shouting in incoherent joy and wrapping her in his arms. Dimly, she was aware of crew members surrounding them and offering congratulations. But it was Greg who filled her mind and heart as he stole a triumphant kiss of celebration.

THE SPIRIT OF THE HOLIDAYS

And now, please enjoy a bonus story
about a girl, a ghost and a Christmas
on the run.
The Spirit of the Holidays
takes place between
Revelations and *Metamorphosis*.

"Aren't you a little bit curious?" Chuck asked. "No one would ever know if I had a look."

Curled up in bed with a warm quilt, Bernie ignored her friend's whispers, watching the trees outside cast shadows on her bedroom window. It didn't feel like Christmas without snow but Mommy said it didn't snow here, not even in the winter. They had to make an adjustment.

"Come on. One tiny peek," Chuck wheedled.

Bernie rolled over to glare at him. "I told you, I want it to be a surprise."

"Okay, don't blow your wig." Chuck wavered, his body going translucent for a moment before solidifying again. "But what if Shawna got you something stupid and educational?"

"Mommy always makes sure I have good

presents. Even when I was in the hospital, she brought me my doll." Bernie hugged the rag doll close. She didn't like remembering the hospital, full of crazy people. It smelled in there, sweaty and stinky, no matter how much they cleaned the rooms. They were mean, insisting that Chuck was a figment of her imagination. Now Mommy and Shawna understood and Bernie didn't have to take the horrible medicine that made her head hurt and her tummy want to throw up.

Her bedroom door opened and Mommy came in. "Hey, Bernie-pie. What are you still doing up?"

"Chuck is being difficult. He won't let me sleep." Bernie sat up in bed.

"I see." Her mother sat down on the bed and ran her cool fingers through Bernie's tangled hair.

"I'm not being difficult!" Chuck shouted.

"Are too!" Bernie shouted back.

"Hey now. It sounds like you two are having a fight. What's wrong?" Mommy tucked Bernie underneath one arm. She was getting too big for cuddles, but it still felt good sometimes.

"He wants to look at my presents," Bernie muttered.

"Chuck, that doesn't sound like the sort of thing that friends do."

Bernie giggled. Mommy was talking to the empty air by the dresser instead of to Chuck, who squatted near the window. He was making faces at her, twisting his mouth with his fingers and sticking out his tongue.

Mommy looked down at her, frowning. Bernie abruptly stopped laughing.

"We had a deal, Chuck. No more telling Bernie to do bad things and getting her into trouble." Mommy lectured the dresser again.

"It's not fair. I just wanted to have a look."

Bernie told her mother what Chuck had said, adding. "But he didn't listen when I said no."

"I see. Can you ask Chuck to come here?"

"He can hear you, Mommy." Bernie waited until Chuck moved closer. "He's beside the bed, near my pillow."

This time Mommy looked in the right direction. "All right. Here's what I think is happening. It's been a long time since you had a Christmas, isn't it, Chuck?"

He nodded sullenly. He'd been dead for a long time. Bernie couldn't quite remember how long, but he remembered still seeing horses on the street instead of cars.

"I bet you miss your family at this time of year," her mother continued.

Chuck crossed his arms and pouted. Bernie looked up at her mother. "But his family was mean to him. They left him all alone."

"Even when family doesn't understand and even when they hurt us, we still miss them,

Bernie-pie. Our hearts don't shut off that easily." Her mother's hug wrapped around her. "But Chuck is forgetting that he's not all alone."

"I'm not?"

"He's not?"

Mommy laughed, a light chuckle that Bernie hadn't heard since she first started talking to Chuck. "There are the families we're born into and then there are the families we find. Chuck is part of our family now. Which is why there's a special present waiting downstairs for him to open in the morning."

"There is?" Chuck started to flicker as if he was going to go peek.

"Stay here. You have to wait until morning. That's the family rules," Bernie scolded.

"She's right, Chuck." Mommy smiled. "And the other part of the family rules is taking care of each other. So you need to let Bernie get a good night's sleep."

Chuck went solid again. "Tell her I will."

Bernie passed on the message.

"Thank you, Chuck. I knew I could count on you." Mommy smiled again and blew a kiss at Chuck. He smiled back, his big mouth stretching even wider.

"Get some rest so that you're both ready for Christmas morning." Mommy tucked Bernie in and gave her a kiss. "Sweet dreams."

After Mommy closed the door, Bernie let her sleepy eyes roll shut.

"Bernie?" Chuck whispered.

"What?" Bernie yawned.

"Do you really think I'm family?"

"Of course you are. You're like my big brother. You're annoying and sometimes we fight, but I still love you and I'd miss you if you were gone." Bernie kept her eyes firmly closed and her hands tucked under the covers.

"I had a big brother." Chuck's voice grew closer and clearer. He was always easier to understand when he calmed down. "He worked at the clip joint down the street. He used to hum these jazz songs and Ma would get mad, sayin' it was disrespectful devil music."

Slumber plucked at Bernie with heavy fingers, lulling her mind into quiet.

"They didn't wait for me."

Bernie's eyes popped open. Chuck sat at the end of her bed, staring toward the window. She sat up. "What?"

He turned to face her, his eyes dark hollows in his face. "After the fire, they didn't wait for me. Ma and Pa moved to San Francisco and Billy got married with some kids. When they died, they didn't come find me."

She didn't know what to say. When the bad people took her last year, it had been super scary and she'd been all alone. But Mommy and the others had kept looking and they'd found her. *Daddy never tried to find you. He just left.* Even before all the really bad stuff, he'd left.

271

"Would you wait for me?" Chuck asked.

That was a question she knew the answer to. "Sure. That's what families do."

"I knew I could count on you, Bernie." He smiled and patted her shoulder, his hand passing right through and leaving cold tingles behind. "Your mom's right. You should sleep. Tomorrow's gonna be a big day."

Car lights flashed across the ceiling and both of them froze. Chuck vanished and Bernie reached down to grab her backpack beside the bed. Before she could pick it up, he reappeared.

"Just a cab dropping off one of the neighbors."

Her chest puffed and deflated in a big sigh. Having to run in the middle of the night sucked. And if they had to do it tonight, she'd have to leave all of her Christmas stuff behind. Then there wouldn't be presents, or cookies for breakfast. Shawna wouldn't sing her French songs and let them sneak butter tarts before dinner. And Mommy would stop laughing.

"Hey, don't worry there, Bernie. I'll keep watch and make sure nobody gets a drop on us." He flickered from the bed to the window, staring out past the tree to the street below.

Bernie curled up under her covers and stared at him, a thin boy with too short pants and suspenders. In the moonlight, he looked as if he were made of glass. She could see through him but he also caught the light around the edges. He wouldn't need to sleep or go to the bathroom. He'd stay there until morning, making sure they were safe. A big yawn crawled out between her lips and she closed her eyes, suddenly too exhausted to do more than whisper. "Thanks, Chuck."

"Don't worry about it, Bernie. It's what families do."

Thank you for reading.

If you enjoyed these stories and have a moment, please leave a review.

It's one of the best ways you can thank an author.

If you're not ready for the fun to end, check out my website www.jclewis.ca for my author commentary.
I share inspirations for my characters and scenes, some of the more interesting bits from my research, and all sorts of other tidbits. Look for the mirror and step on through…

You can also sign up for my newsletter to find out about new releases, my author events and get bonus scenes and other insider information.

Sign up at www.jclewis.ca.

ACKNOWLEDGEMENTS:

Even a short story requires many people besides the author.

Thank you again to my critique partner, Chris and to Cait Gordon of Dynamic Canvas editing. Both of them helped to polish my stories into their best possible form.

Writing the *Spirit Sight* short stories has been a lot of fun. I hope you enjoyed them.

Thank you to Samianne for the amazing covers and awesome interstitial illustration.

As always, my final thank you is to the reader. Without you, there is no book, only me musing to myself. Thanks for taking a jaunt into my world.

ABOUT THE AUTHOR

Image copyright © Ryan Parent

Jennifer Carole Lewis is a full-time mom, a full-time administrator and a full-time writer, which means she is very much interested in speaking to anyone who comes up with any form of functional time-travel devices or practical cloning methods. Meanwhile, she spends her most of her time alternating between organizing and typing.

She is a devoted comic book geek and Marvel movie enthusiast. She spends far too much of her precious free time watching TV, especially police procedural dramas. Her enthusiasm outstrips her talent in karaoke, cross-stitch and jigsaw puzzles. She is a voracious reader of a wide variety of fiction and non-fiction and always enjoys seeking out new suggestions.

She has been making up stories since before she could read and write. This is what she's always wanted to do. Thank you for making her dream come true.

For more information about *Spirit Sight* (including behind-the-scenes commentary), more books on the *lalassu* and her blog, you can go to www.jclewis.ca. Check out her monthly blog features: Heroine Fix, a look at the strong and intriguing heroines who inspire me, and Hidden Diamonds, a monthly feature on her fellow authors who write strong women, paranormal romance and romantic suspense. You can also find Jennifer on:

> Facebook (Jennifer Carole Lewis)
> Twitter (@jclewisupdate)
> Instagram (jennifer_carole_lewis)

Or you can even sign up for her newsletter on her website and get all of the inside information, including bonus/deleted scenes and casting photos for upcoming books.